A Homecoming Ménage Christmas

The Key Club #7

Jan Springer

RACHEL HAS A VERY NAUGHTY secret and she's way too embarrassed to let anyone know about it. When The Key Club throws a Santa Fetish Ménage Night, it's almost too good to be true. She has to figure out how to participate without anyone finding out!

Key Club bartenders Rob and Ron have fallen head over Santa hats for quiet, nice girl Rachel. But she has no clue how they feel about her. But she will know, because Rachel is coming home from a trip to Europe and the two men are going to give her the best Homecoming Ménage Christmas ever. They'll do it with the help of some naughty toys, the Red Room, a safe word and...Santa Claus.

Newsletter

Hi! If you would like to get an email when my books are released, you can sign up here:

Newsletter: http://ymlp.com/xguembmugmgb

Your emails will never be shared and you can unsubscribe whenever you like.

A Homecoming Ménage Christmas

Published by Spunky Girl Publishing

1st edition
Cover by Melody Simmons ~ Ebook Indie Covers
Edited by Julie Naughton

Author Note

This is a work of fiction. Characters, places, settings, and events presented in this book are purely of the author's imagination and bear no resemblance to any actual person, living or dead or to any actual events, places, and/or settings.

Prologue

DEAR DIARY,

I have a Santa Claus fetish. That's my biggest secret. Only you can ever know, except of course for a couple of boyfriends who just didn't like dressing up as Santa out of season. They said I was immature, weird and totally off the wall wanting to be made love to by Santa Claus. I wish I was normal just like everybody else.

She closed the diary she'd inadvertently discovered in Rachel's bedroom and frowned.

Wow, she'd had no idea Rachel was into Santa. She'd heard about women who got turned on by the red-and-black clad, white-bearded guy but...sweet and quiet Rachel?

She would never have guessed. Not in a million years.

She placed the diary back beneath the cushion of the chair by Rachel's writing desk. She hadn't meant to pry, truly she hadn't. She'd just been doing the housecleaning for Rachel's homecoming and she'd found her diary purely by accident.

She *should* have left it alone, but she was curious by nature and hadn't been able to resist flipping through the entries until she'd stopped at the Santa Claus fetish entry. How in the world was she going to help Rachel without her finding out that she now knew about her Santa fetish?

She frowned and went about her cleaning.

Chapter One

SEVERAL DAYS LATER...

"Who are you again?"

Raw emotions bubbled inside Rachel's chest as she stared at her father. He sat like a rag doll in his wheelchair. His gray hair was in disarray and a stream of drool dribbled from the sides of his mouth. Normally she'd comb his hair, wash his face, brush his teeth and then read to him. But today she was just too tired to do anything, and she was so incredibly sad at how his life would end. As he looked up at her there was no hint of recognition in his pale blue eyes. No clue that she was his daughter.

"Dad," she whispered and attempted a smile. It was seriously wobbly.

"My name is Rachel," she said in a louder voice. *Please remember me, Dad.*

She extended her hand. He hesitated before placing his limp, cold fingers against her palm. They shook hands. His grip was weaker than yesterday, and even weaker than the day before.

"Are you the nurse?" he asked softly.

Oh, God, no.

"No, Dad. I'm your daughter, remember?"

A surge of hope swelled through her as acknowledgement flared in his eyes. Just as quickly, the recognition faded. Utter despair embraced her.

"Hello. Do I know you?" he asked again. That absent look was back again.

Dad, please. I need you back.

Rachel sighed. "No, you don't know me. I'll drop in again tomorrow. Bye for now."

She should stay and spend some time with him, but all she wanted to do was go home, crawl into bed, pull the blankets over her head and just sleep the rest of her life away.

Bitter tears bubbled up and after she passed the several wheelchairs riddled with elderly people, she let the hot tears roll.

Damn you, Dad.

RACHEL AWOKE TO THE sound of the pilot announcing they would soon be landing and to please put on seatbelts. She did as instructed and ignored the little old lady who sat beside her and smiled sympathetically at her.

Her dad had died that night. All alone. In his sleep. The guilt of not spending time with him that day and not being there when he'd passed had gnawed at her so bad that her friends had footed the bill and sent her off on a trip to Europe.

Rachel smiled and her heart warmed as she remembered the elderly widows her friends had sent her to. One in Italy. One in France. The other in Switzerland. They'd been kind to her and had kept her busy, teaching her how to cook, how to style her hair and how to make homemade wine.

Now, after several months abroad, she was on her way home. Back to her hometown and to all her friends who'd supported her. Guilt still lingered about her dad and her sadness over time had turned a little less intense. She was going home. Back to where her dad had passed away. Back to the memories.

Rachel shook her head. No, she had to stop thinking like this. She'd done her best for her father. The realization had hit her when she'd been on a gondola in Venice and she'd watched a woman around her age helping her elderly fragile father into the boat. Dark circles hugged the woman's eyes, but she smiled as the elderly gentleman had smiled back at her. Dad had been happy while he'd still been with her. Until his last shred of memories had gone. He'd been happy and she'd done her best.

That's all that mattered. Now it was her turn to be happy.

"I DON'T SEE RACHEL. Are you sure she's coming in on this flight?" Rob asked his twin brother as they stood near the arrival gates, watching the people picking up their luggage at the turnstile.

"That's what it said in the email from Jaxie. See?" Ron held up the paper.

"Yep, no mistake. So where is she?"

"Maybe she got by us somehow?" Ron replied as he tried to see past the crush of passengers who were now piling through the doors.

Man, he couldn't wait to see her. He'd barely been able to get to know her when his brother and he had been hired at the Key Club as bartenders. They'd worked with Rachel and had fallen hard for the quiet woman. Then her dad passed away, and she'd gotten way too sad. No one had been able to cheer her up. Not even them.

"Fuck, there she is," Rob suddenly said in a low, thick voice that sent a shard of frustration through Ron. Where? He couldn't see her. But then his brother pointed to a sexy-looking woman, and then his entire world suddenly slipped into place.

There. She was picking up her two suitcases. She looked...different. He could barely recognize her. She had a new hairdo. Shorter than when she'd left. Instead of auburn, it looked lighter in color and she also had some cute blue streaks running through the strands. She wore wide gold loop earrings and an elegant knee-length ivory dress with gold buttons down the entire front. Her shoes were white too. Not the best for walking on an icy Alberta road, though. He wished he'd brought some warm boots and a snug coat for her.

"She's beautiful," Rob muttered. Awe edged his voice.

Ron shook his head. "What? You sound surprised. She's always been beautiful, asshole."

"Yeah, but before she was tired, worn out, like a wilting flower. She's blossomed. Matured."

Ron's heart sped up as he watched Rachel approach the exit. She hadn't seen them yet. She looked refreshed. The vacation in Europe had been just what she needed. He was glad they'd all pitched in for her trip.

But even more, he was glad she was back.

Rachel's mouth dropped open the instant she saw them.

Ron and Rob Simpson. Good grief. What in the world were they doing here? They were twin brothers who'd worked with her at the Key Club. At first she hadn't been able to tell them apart. But then she'd realized that Ron's smile was just a bit wider than Rob's and that Rob's shoulders were just a touch broader than his brother's.

Her heart picked up a mad pace. They looked...hot. She hadn't seen them in almost seven months. As she watched them looking into the crowd, she realized she'd missed them like crazy. She'd been drawn to them the instant Jaxie had hired them. They'd been fun and sweet and they had come on to her like crazy. But then her dad had died...

Rachel frowned as a fresh wave of sadness clutched her. She didn't want to go into the past. She just wanted to go forward now.

She liked them. A lot. But the last thing she needed right now was their sweetness. She just wanted...them. *Both of them.*

Rachel groaned inwardly. Why hadn't Jaxie come to pick her up like she'd promised? Maybe she should just try to sneak past them? The last thing she wanted to do was to deal with her feelings for them.

"Hey, beautiful!" Ron called out to her the instant she breezed through the doorway.

Shoot! Caught!

"How's our favorite boss lady tonight? Enjoy your trip, beautiful?" Rob asked as he quickly grabbed her suitcases from her. Ron's warm hand splayed across her lower back and he guided her though the crowd and out the door.

She shivered as the icy December wind bit into her. Wow, she'd forgotten how cold a Canadian winter could be. Ron must have noticed her reaction for within a few seconds he'd removed his lambswool-lined leather jacket and draped it over her shoulders.

They had a taxi and driver waiting and Ron quickly opened the door, ushering her in. It was warm inside and as Ron sat down beside her, it got warmer. Seconds later, Rob jumped in and she heard the driver slam the trunk closed.

"We missed you, boss lady," Ron smiled. His white teeth flashed in the dark interior and his eyes twinkled with a happiness that surprised her. He really had missed her. She'd missed him too. Both of them.

"Too damned much," Rob chuckled. To her surprise, Rob draped an arm over her shoulders and pulled her against him, squeezing her tight.

"Hey, quit hogging the woman," his brother complained. His broad shoulder pressed against Rachel's and his palm slid against hers. He clenched his fingers around hers.

Wow. Sandwiched between two sexy hunks. How interesting.

After the taxi driver stepped into the vehicle Rob gave him her address, and the brothers filled her in on what was happening at the Key Club. The owner of the club, Jaxie — who just happened to be Rachel's best friend — was having a baby, and she was due in a couple of weeks. Jaxie's two men, Ewan and Royce, appeared nervous and excited every time one or the other dropped into work to pick Jaxie up and take her home.

Rachel grinned as Ron and Rob took turns bringing her up to speed on their mutual friends. She already knew what was going on because she and Jaxie had spoken often while Rachel had been in Europe. Jaxie didn't know the sex of her baby, as they'd decided to let it be a surprise. While Rachel been away, the Club had gotten even more popular. With Rachel returning to take over for Jaxie, she'd been told she would have her hands full running the place when Jaxie went on leave. Thankfully, Jaxie had hired several new employees to help out.

"And best of all, the Key Club is having a Santa Fetish Ménage Night this coming Saturday."

Rob's words rocked her world.

Santa Fetish? And ménage? Jaxie had not mentioned this tidbit of information.

She grabbed onto the thread of conversation as if it were a lifeline.

"What was that?" she asked, pretending she hadn't heard.

To her surprise, her voice sounded bedroom breathy.

Girl! Rein in your excitement!

"Yeah, Jaxie said that someone dropped the idea into the club's suggestion box, so she ran with it. Says she wanted something different for this Christmas," Ron said. His eyes narrowed as he peered at her.

"Why? Are you interested in a ménage?"

Her mouth went dry. They didn't know the half of it.

Say no. Walk...no...run from this conversation. Do it now before they catch on that you have a Santa fetish.

"I might be," she replied trying like hell to keep her voice impersonal when her insides were absolutely bursting with anticipation.

"It does sound like fun," Rob replied with a grin.

But when they said nothing else, disappointment pummelled her.

Ron fell silent as well. But the taxi driver was glancing at her in the rearview mirror. Had he picked up on her excitement?

Her thoughts whirled. Jaxie was throwing a Santa fetish night and Rachel could hardly wait! She had to be included.

Another thought rocked her. Now that Rachel was back in town, Jaxie was expecting her to take over running The Key Club while she went on maternity leave. What if she had to work *that* night?

Darn. She needed to figure out a way to get her Santa fix. And a ménage. *Wow, two fantasies in one!*

The guys continued talking, filling her in on the holiday events going on in town, but she tuned them out as visions of Santa Claus began to dance in her head.

"WOULD YOU GUYS LIKE to come in for some hot chocolate?" Rachel asked a few minutes later as Rob and Ron, with her luggage in tow, walked her to her front door.

Someone, most likely Jaxie, had left a sweet garland wreath, laden with tiny red bows and golden bells, hanging on her front door. And strings of blinking red miniature lights had been draped over several of the smaller snow-clad pine trees that edged the front of her house. It looked quite Christmasy.

"Actually we would love to—"

Before Rob could finish, his brother interrupted him.

"But we have somewhere else to go tonight."

Disappointment melted through her. She'd wanted to repay them in some small way for meeting her at the airport.

"Okay. Well, thanks so much for coming to get me. That was awfully sweet of the two of you."

Rob grinned. "We're really glad you're back and you're looking healthy."

"Fresh Austrian alps air, Italian wine, Swiss chocolate and French cuisine helped. Thanks to all you guys," Rachel replied. A sudden pang of missing Europe breathed through her. Wouldn't it be great to go back there with Ron and Rob and show them all the attractions she'd seen?

For a wonderful few seconds, happiness brushed her senses. She gasped at the intensity of it and remembered that the only lights in her dark world while she'd been going through her father's illness had been Jaxie, and then toward the end, Rob and Ron.

"So? We'll see you at work then?" Ron suddenly asked. He'd moved onto the porch with her. He smelled really nice. Better than any man she'd ever known. Rob smelled just as nice as he joined Ron and crowded in beside her too.

Rob took the key from her hand, and a moment later, her door was open and her suitcases inside.

To her surprise, both men leaned toward her and kissed her tenderly on each of her cheeks. The intimate press of their warm lips and their raspy five-o'clock shadows made her toes curl.

My. Yes, very nice, guys.

"Until we meet again, my sweet," Rob whispered. His green eyes sparkled, and for a second, Rachel thought he was going to kiss her again. On her mouth this time. To her surprise, she really wanted him to. Her lips tingled with want and she parted them with anticipation, not really caring if Ron was watching. Heck, he could kiss her too if he wanted.

"I'll need my jacket back and you need to get in before you catch a cold," Ron whispered.

She'd been so warm tucked away in his coat that she'd forgotten it was still draped over her shoulders!

Rachel allowed him to slip it off her shoulders and then she stepped into her open doorway, thankful that a lovely blast of warm air embraced her from inside.

Both men waved, turned and strolled down the snowy stairs into the swirling flurries. They walked quickly toward the taxi. Just before they got inside, they both waved again and she waved back.

Gosh, suddenly she hated for them to go. A blast of frigid air blew into the doorway, and she shivered, yet stayed in the doorway until she couldn't see the red lights of the vehicle anymore. Then glanced across the street to Jaxie's house. Pretty blue Christmas lights twinkled beneath a dusting of snow where they'd been draped over her hedges and a Christmas tree with similar blue lights stood just inside the living room window. But the indoor lights were off.

Either Jaxie was already in bed with her two men, or she was over at the Key Club working. Had she forgotten that Rachel was flying in tonight? Was that why Jaxie hadn't picked her up as promised?

Rachel frowned. Maybe Jaxie had gone into early labor? She hoped everything was all right with the baby. As she stepped inside her house, the familiarity of being back here without her dad, punched her in the gut.

Tears bubbled and her vision blurred.

She was alone. So alone.

Shoot. She needed to get a grip. She couldn't cave the instant she came back home. She spied the light blinking on her answering machine and hurried to check for messages. There were several welcome-home messages, and then one from Jaxie stating she was sorry she hadn't been able to make it to pick her up tonight. She hadn't been able to get someone to cover for her at the club.

Rachel shook her head. Why hadn't Jaxie called and left a message on Rachel's cell phone? Why leave a message here? And she was the boss. How could she not get someone to cover for her tonight?

Well, it didn't matter. As long as Jaxie was all right, then all was good. Her best friend was so lucky that she had found not one but two guys to take care of her. That's what Rachel craved. Someone in her life to protect her, to love her and just to take care of her so she wouldn't have to worry about everything anymore.

It would have been nice to come home to family. Yet here she was, alone. But she was lucky. She was in a much better place mentally and physically than she'd been before she'd gone away. So much better.

She'd just have to hold onto that thought and she would be okay.

"UNTIL WE MEET AGAIN, my sweet?" Ron chuckled as he and Rob watched Rachel's two-story house disappear in a swirl of snowflakes.

"Well, she is sweet," Rob defended.

"Yeah, sweet as sin."

"Sinfully delicious," Rob added with a dreamy look.

Ron rolled his eyes. Geez, his brother was as smitten with Rachel as he. They'd been attracted to the same girl in the past. When it had happened the first several times, they'd fought each other like wild dogs. They'd tried to get the girlfriend the other had. But it had always ended badly because the girl wanted nothing to do with their rivalry.

To make things worse, one or the other would end up with a broken nose, or bruised ribs or something else broken. They'd taken a period of time where they'd lived apart and not seen each other, but that hadn't lasted.

They were twins. They needed each other like they required to breathe air. So, they'd ended up friends again, needing each other to survive. They'd moved to this town because they'd heard of the Key Club and their Ménage Nights. It was the perfect opportunity to introduce themselves to a lady who just might want to be shared. Not just for one night, but forever.

But before they'd had their chance to indulge in a ménage, they'd met Rachel. She was a quiet woman. Sweet and so damned sexy that they swore she had no idea how sexy she truly was to them. She'd ruined them for any other woman. They only wanted Rachel, but her life had spiralled into turmoil and he'd stuck to the idea that good things came to those who waited. Now Rachel was back and she made Ron feel like he was the luckiest man in the world.

"Penny for your thoughts, little brother," Rob whispered.

"You're only one minute older, big man."

Rob chuckled. "Yeah, but oldest gets first dibs on when we introduce ourselves to Rachel, and by her reaction about Santa Fetish Night, I'd say she wants a ménage and we'll be seeing more of her that particular night. So much more."

"So, you noticed her reaction as well. She tried to cover it, but I could see it in her eyes. The excitement. The need."

"If sexual excitement was a block of hot air, we could have cut right into it with a knife," Rob replied.

"Or my hard cock," Ron muttered beneath his breath so only his brother could hear. He shifted uneasily on the cab seat, trying to loosen the tightness of his pants strangling his twitching shaft.

"There's just something magnetic about her," Rob said softly.

Ron nodded. "I sure as hell don't mind dressing up like Santa for Rachel on Santa Fetish night. Hell, I would do if for her any time of the year."

By the naughty grin on his brother's face, he clearly was interested in Santa dress up as well.

Chapter Two

FROM HER BED, RACHEL stared at the icy snowflakes that pelted her bedroom window. She'd slept straight through the night. Jet lag did that. Made her snooze like a rock. But her sleep had been filled with naughty dreams of Rob and Ron. Of them touching her in the most intimate of ways.

Instantly, her breaths came faster as she remembered how she'd dreamed of them appearing in her bedroom. Both wore Santa hats and nothing else but their birthday suits. Their cocks were long and thick and they'd stroked their shafts as they'd stared down at her.

And then they'd climbed into bed with her...

Rachel exhaled at the raw intensity of the intimate things they'd done to her. Just remembering how aroused she'd been while in her dreams, made her slide her hands over her sensitive breasts. She moaned softly as she tweaked and pinched her nipples and allowed her thoughts to drift back to the scorching dreams.

"Come on, baby. Spread your luscious legs. Give us a good look at your sweet pussy," Ron whispered as he stood at the foot of her bed. His voice was a velvet magnet, stroking her senses.

Without hesitation she pushed aside her covers, widened her legs and slipped a hand between her thighs.

"Succulent," Rob whispered. He stood beside his brother at the foot of her bed as they watched her touch herself. Their Santa hats perched precariously over their heads.

Gosh, they looked ultra-sexy wearing those red and white hats.

"I want a taste," Ron said.

An instant later, he climbed onto the mattress. His engorged cock bobbed gently as he lowered himself and then nestled his body between her thighs. His shoulders were oh-so-wide as they pushed her thighs even farther apart. To accommodate him, she lifted her feet and dug her heels into the strong muscles of his lower back. She gazed down at him and he stared back at her with bright-green eyes.

"You belong to us now, Rachel," he whispered.

She shivered with anticipation as Ron licked his red lips and lowered his head. In a split second, she was awash in sensations as he lapped his tongue against her pussy.

Beside her, Rob lay upon the bed, his head dipping toward her chest. She reached out and tangled her fingers into his silky hair, guiding his head to her breast. His hot lips sucked her left nipple into his moist mouth. A hand palmed her other breast and he massaged her sensitive flesh.

Ron's tongue caressed and massaged and kissed her clitoris. Rachel's breaths came faster and she grew hotter as her clit pulsed with arousal. She tightened her thighs around Ron's head, squeezing.

His licks became more intense, turning into wicked laps and harsh sucks on her labia.

Rob began pulling on her nipple with his teeth, until pricks of pleasure-pain snapped through her.

She gasped as Ron plunged a couple of fingers into her wet pussy, then withdrew. He began a fast pump into her vagina.

Rob's mouth lashed her nipple, his hand massaging her sensitive breast.

Oddly, their Santa hats remained on their heads and the sight turned her on so much, she could barely stand the onslaught of erotic quivers rocking her.

Her breaths came faster, her thighs clenched. The sultry storm of sensations came fast and furious, raging through her and ripping away any self-control. She undulated, loving the wild tremors ripping into her. She arched her back, pressed her breasts harder against Rob's hands and mouth.

Adrenaline rushed through her. She bucked against the convulsions and cried out as lightning forces exploded and tore her thoughts and body apart.

The climax was never ending and when she finally went slack and felt drained, she smiled.

Wow! She really needed to participate in that Santa Fetish Ménage Night. She just had to figure out how to get herself involved without anyone recognizing her.

"MY GOODNESS, LADIES! I am so sorry for being so late. And Rachel! I apologize for not picking you up at the airport last night," Jaxie gushed as she burst into the private dining room at the restaurant where Rachel and Jewel were chatting about what adult toys would be appropriate for The Key Club's Santa Fetish Ménage Night.

Rachel had been out doing grocery shopping late this morning when Jaxie had called and left a message for Rachel to meet Jaxie and Jewel at the local restaurant for an impromptu business meetings concerning the Santa Fetish Ménage Night.

Of course, Rachel had arrived way too early. Thankfully, Jewel, the woman who supplied the Key Club with adult toys had shown up. They'd already started taking a look at the catalogs that Jewel had brought along.

Rachel grinned as Jaxie shrugged off her heavy winter jacket. Her cheeks and nose were red from the wintry Alberta cold and her eyes snapped with an excitement that sifted through Rachel like bolts of lightning. Jaxie's exuberant attitude about life in general was something that had always attracted Rachel to her friend. This time was no exception.

Jaxie was beaming as she gazed at Jewel and then at Rachel.

"Royce and Ewan refused to let me leave the house to come and get you at the airport because of the snow. They practically tied me to our bed," Jaxie stopped and giggled and then lowered her voice.

"Actually, they *did* tie me to the bed. Let me tell you that those two naughty men are quite creative in the ways of pleasuring a very pregnant woman." She rubbed her very swollen belly and sat down on the empty chair they'd reserved for her.

"Don't worry about it. Rob and Ron picked me up and got me home," Rachel admitted and reached out to touch Jaxie's belly.

Jewel and Jaxie exchanged surprised looks and suddenly Rachel got the feeling that maybe Jaxie hadn't sent them to pick her up.

"My gosh, have you ever grown since that last selfie you sent me," Rachel said and laughed. It was incredible that this was happening to Jaxie. A woman who'd at one point in her life had not wanted a family, due to her own tragic past.

Jaxie smiled proudly as she stared down at where Rachel rubbed her big belly.

"Yeah, the kid was an accident, but the best accident of my life. But I want to know about Ron and Ron. They picked you up? Really?"

Okay, surprise like that couldn't be faked. Could it?

"You didn't ask them?"

Jaxie shrugged her shoulders. "No. I figured you'd grab a taxi if you didn't see me. You know how I get when I'm working. I lose all track of time."

"If you didn't, then who did send them?" Rachel asked.

"I'm not sure. I mean I told everyone I was going to pick you up. The only two who knew I wasn't going to make it were Ewan and Royce and they don't strike me as matchmakers."

"Maybe Rob and Ron just wanted to be there to welcome you home? Maybe they missed you," Jewel said softly.

"They did ask about you all the time. But I didn't tell them how to reach you. I figured this was your time and you needed space," Jaxie said in a casual voice as she leisurely flipped through one of the toy catalogs.

A tremble of excitement shifted through Rachel, not only because Ron and Rob might be interested in her but arousal at the glimpses of Santa-themed adult toys in the catalog.

"Those boys are cute. They do have quite the large muscles on them," Jaxie continued. "Very strong-looking arms with large hands and long fingers."

Rachel bit her bottom lip as visions of Ron and Rob fluttered inside her mind. Their hands wrapped around Santa vibes, plunging the toys in and out of her pussy and ass as she climaxed over and over.

Mercy! It *was* getting warm in here. She reached for the tall glass of ice-cube-laden water on the table. Suddenly she wished she could run one of those cubes over her face or better yet, all over her hot chest!

"Here's a really hot line of Christmas toys," Jewel said as she settled an open binder in front of Rachel.

There were sizzling pictures of Santa-clad sexy men. Some had their cocks dressed in candy cane socks or they wore reindeer and Santa hats. One model wore a condom with a mistletoe on top of his cock.

Oh boy.

Jewel gazed over at Rachel and winked. "All these items with a Santa theme are adorable, aren't they?"

Rachel's cheeks began to heat and betray her.

Man! Did Jewel know about her Santa fetish? Is that why she'd winked? Her heart went into a maddening speed. Oh why! Why did she have to have this problem of being incredibly attracted to men dressed up like Santa?

By the time their business brunch was over, Rachel could barely stand the arousal coursing through her. And she had to go to work after leaving here! Jaxie wanted her back to the Club and take over the helm because her two men were now insisting that with Rachel back in town, Jaxie should start to work only half-days.

"You were awfully quiet in the restaurant. Is something wrong?" Jaxie asked as she unlocked the back door to the Club and they hurried in out of the frigid cold.

"No, just getting reacquainted with the weather," Rachel lied. For dramatic effect, she yanked off her gloves and began blowing on her hands, pretending her fingers were cold. They were anything but cold. All of her was...hot.

She needed relief. Needed to get the pictures of all those Santa-themed toys out of her freaking head.

"You got spoiled in Europe, didn't you?" Jaxie laughed as they removed their coats and boots and stuffed them into a closet.

"It really was nice. I feel much better now. I think I can face the world again," Rachel admitted as she followed Jaxie down the hall.

She'd expected them to go into Jaxie's office, which Rachel assumed she'd be using now. Instead, Jaxie motioned for her to follow her farther down the hall. She stopped a couple of doors down in front of the room where they kept office and cleaning supplies.

But the instant Jaxie opened the door, Rachel's mouth dropped open in surprise. It was as if she'd been transported into some fancy, modern office room. Gone was the clutter of cleaning supplies, cleaning carts, and the bookshelf that had been overflowing with office supplies. Instead of the room smelling musty, it smelled fresh and clean. The walls had been covered with a red-brick-style paneling, and in a corner was a freestanding red electric fireplace. The orange glow of coals and flickering of realistic flames made Rachel feel so warm and embraced.

"Jaxie? What have you done? Did you get yourself a new office?" Rachel asked softly as Jaxie motioned for her to come inside the room.

As Jaxie closed the door behind them, Rachel gazed at the old-fashioned roll-top desk against the far wall.

She'd always wanted one of these old desks, and now Jaxie had one in her new office. Lucky girl.

"For you, Rach. You'll be the new boss while I'm gone, so you need a nice nook to take care of business. My office is just too messy, and I could never part with it. So I figured that since you'll be a permanent figure here, you'll need your own office."

My own office? What? Shock snapped through her and Rachel covered her mouth and shook her head. Disbelief wrapped around her.

"No way. Not for me. But it's so fancy." She loved bricks, and her favorite color was red. This was gorgeous. Even the lone window had sweet white lace that had been pulled to the side with big puffy bows. The window gave her a view to the front of the club and the snow-drenched pine trees that bordered the property as well as the gorgeous Rocky Mountains in the background.

"Nothing is too fancy for my best friend," Jaxie laughed. She moved over to the desk, rolled up the roll-top and revealed an array of cubbyholes.

Wow. Nice.

"Look, tons of places for you to put your pens, pencils, and stapler and..." Jaxie hesitated as her gaze dropped to the desktop. Rachel gasped as she spied the miniature Santa Claus keychain with a key on it.

"Isn't this cute. The guys must have put the office key onto this keychain," Jaxie said. She lay her cell phone on the desk, lifted the small three-inch tall Santa with dangling key and Rachel's breath caught and her pussy quivered.

Shit. Was someone onto her? Or was she just getting paranoid?

A sharp knock at the door made Rachel jump and Jaxie grinned curiously at her reaction.

"Hey, Jaxie! Are you in there?" A familiar voice shot through the door. Was that Rob? Or Ron? She simply couldn't tell by voice alone.

"We're here. Come on in," Jaxie called out. She placed the tiny Santa back on the desk and stepped out of the way a second before the door swung inward and almost knocked into her.

"Did you see the—" he stopped short when he spied Rachel. A huge grin swept over his sweet mouth and suddenly Rachel had an overwhelming urge to kiss him. Or be kissed, just as she'd had the other night on her porch.

Crap, why was she reacting so much? Heck, she knew why. Eons without sex and a bunch of Santa toys to ogle over at brunch.

"Hey, boss lady," he said to Rachel. "Didn't know you were here. So, I guess you saw the desk. How do you ladies like it?"

Okay, this was Ron. She could tell by that sexy little mole on the left side of his mouth. Rob didn't have one there, did he? She couldn't remember. Ron kept his gaze glued to her when he asked the question, but Jaxie quickly answered.

"It's perfect for Rachel. So many cubbyholes for all her knickknacks."

"Yeah, I remember you mentioning that fetish," he answered.

Fetish?

"I see you found the little Santa," Ron said as he spied the Santa keychain. "Rob saw it and thought it would be perfect for the holidays and for Rachel."

Okay, was it her imagination, or had Ron's voice suddenly turned husky?

Oh boy.

"Yeah, I thought it fit the season," Rob said as he strolled into the room.

In a flash, Jaxie pushed between the two guys and headed for the open door.

"You guys did a fantastic job. But you know what? I need to grab my stuff and get out of here. Ewan and Royce are expecting me home earlier tonight and I don't like to keep my guys waiting. See you all later. Have fun!"

And then Jaxie was gone. It had happened so fast, it took Rachel a good half a minute to realize she was alone with the two of them.

Suddenly the room seemed way too small for the three of them. And way too quiet.

"Alone at last," Rob murmured.

The soft sound of his voice instantly captured Rachel's attention. The lusty expressions on both men's faces made her very aware that something different was happening between them. Gone were the sweet, sexy men she knew before she'd left for Europe. They'd been replaced by husky, dominating guys who suddenly towered over her.

A shivery tension of awareness zipped through her. She wasn't used to such closeness from these men. It made her a tad nervous, yet tremendously curious as well.

"Um, thanks for getting all this together for me. I really appreciate it," Rachel stopped as Ron's expression darkened. Yep, something very hot was happening, and it was time to leave.

"Um, I need to get out front and check on some stuff..." Yeah, she needed to leave here because instincts told her if she didn't go, then something naughty was going to happen to her.

"Rachel," Ron grabbed her elbow as she tried to squeeze by the two brothers. She gasped as his grip tightened.

His gaze was serious.

"We really did miss you when you were gone. Both of us did," he whispered.

Both of them?

What in the world was he insinuating? She really should stop whatever was happening. But she felt magnetized to him. To both of them. Oh wow, what were they going to do to her? In here?

"Guys..." she whispered.

"Shh, let us pleasure you," Rob whispered as he moved in behind her.

Pleasure me? What the...

Rob pressed himself against her backside and her throat went dry. The distinct impression of an erection pushing against the crack of her ass made her tremble.

She whimpered in obedience and instinctively pressed her butt against him.

He groaned softly. Her eyes widened with surprise at her behavior.

She should be fighting this. Fighting her submissive response to their overwhelming dominance.

Instead, her resolve weakened as Ron let go of her elbow and reached up to caress her right cheek with the back of his hand. Instinctively, she moved into his gentle touch.

Chapter Three

HIS HAND LEFT HER FACE and she gasped as his fingers dipped beneath the hem of her skirt and her blouse was tugged free and lifted.

"We want you, Rachel," Ron breathed.

Surprise rocked her.

We? Me? No, this is not happening. Am I having another dream?

Ron's warm hands splayed against her bare tummy. Rachel's belly muscles clenched. She creamed.

She closed her eyes as Ron's head lowered and she whimpered as his warm mouth melted over hers, not gently as she'd expected, but hot and forceful. Possessive.

"You are beautiful, Rachel," Rob mumbled into her ear. She tensed as his hot breath caressed her cheek and he sucked her left earlobe between his lips.

Tingles rippled along her spine.

Goodness! Things were happening so fast that they weren't even registering in her mind. But it sure had the rest of her reacting. She loved how Ron caressed his lips along hers, and the fact that Rob was hiking her skirt above her waist. Her undies suddenly were pulled past her thighs and down her legs, puddling at her ankles. But Rob didn't let her panties sit there for long, as he urged her to step out of them.

She stood before them, naked below her waist. Her exposure to them excited her. She kissed Ron back. Loved her unfamiliar aggression of wanting more from *both* of them.

"Spread your legs for me, baby," Rob said from behind her. From the angle of his voice near her waist she knew he'd dropped to his knees.

She hesitated, her mind awhirl with confusion. Was this happening? She couldn't get her bearings.

She went with her instincts and widened her stance.

"That's a girl," Rob whispered.

A moment later, hot air blew against her pussy. Rachel gasped and creamed.

"Gorgeous pussy," Rob breathed.

A finger swept over her sensitive clit. Rob rubbed her until she was moaning into Ron's mouth, her body aflame with arousal and her breaths rushing fast and heavy. Suddenly, Ron broke their kiss and as she blinked her eyes open, she saw his swollen red mouth and lust-lidded eyes.

"I need a taste of you," he whispered in a hoarse voice.

Rachel nodded numbly. She thought he meant he was going to go down on her as Rob was now doing. But Rob was down there. Her thoughts continued to swirl in confusion.

Ron's heated hands moved up along her belly and dipped beneath her breasts. He lifted her bra and as Ron dipped his head toward her breast, she caught sight of the little red Santa that Jaxie had placed in one of the desk's cubbyholes. It was standing, facing her. It was only a few feet away, watching them.

Rachel gasped as her vagina and breasts suddenly became awash with red-hot lightning pleasure bolts. A moment later, Ron enclosed her left nipple with his mouth and Rob covered her pussy with his lips. His tongue dipped between her labia and he thrust into her vagina like a miniature cock.

She continued to stare at the Santa figure. A fever swept through her. Tremors and sensations rocked her and stole her breath. She clenched her thighs against Rob's head. He moaned and slurped at her clit and then sucked at her vagina opening, igniting more pleasure.

Ron cupped her breasts, squeezing and massaging as his hot lips pulled sweetly on her nipple until pleasure-pain sizzled.

Rob caressed her ass cheeks, his teeth tugging at her labia, his frantic mouth slurping and licking, and she fought to keep her keening to a dull roar.

She was out of control, her breaths catching at the incredible arousal gushing into her. She thrashed her head back and forth, gyrated her hips and thrust her hands onto Ron's shoulders as his mouth moved to her other breast.

As she continued to stare at Santa, she imagined the jolly bearded fellow as being here, his mouth on her breasts and pussy. Fevered desperation fused into her.

Rachel gyrated harder against Rob's head. Pleasure overwhelmed her. Her mind shattered, the splinters of thoughts a million colored pieces. It was beautiful. Spectacular.

All too soon the spasms ebbed and she fought to control her frantic panting.

What had just happened?

Her body purred with satisfaction. Need throbbed through her. She wanted them to do this to her again. Over and over.

She wanted more. Wanted them thrusting their cocks into her. Tension swiftly built again and she whimpered her distress.

Santa stared back at her. She swore the figurine winked.

Goodness! Now she was hallucinating?

Rob stopped slurping and Ron suddenly pulled away. "Someone's coming," Ron whispered.

"Rachel? Are you still in your office?"

Jaxie's voice froze Rachel.

Oh no!

Rob chuckled and he dropped her leg from the desk. Rachel blinked with shock. When had he placed her leg up on the desk in the first place?

Ron slowly moved away and grinned.

"Your skirt is hiked," he whispered.

Shit! Rachel managed to kick her panties under the desk and drop her skirt an instant before Jaxie knocked one more time and then entered.

If she was surprised to see the three of them in the office, she didn't show it. But surely Jaxie could see how red her cheeks were getting?

"Listen, I forgot that I left my cellphone here on your desk. I was looking all over for it. In my office, out in my car and then I remembered I left it here," Jaxie said as she picked up the cell and pocketed it. "The guys don't want me to bring it home as I keep a lot of my contact info on it, but hey, I'm pregnant, not dead, right?"

She laughed and grinned at Rachel.

"Are you all right, hon? You look a bit flushed."

Rachel's cheeks heated even more and her lips were really tingling from Ron's kiss. Thankfully, Ron came to Rachel's rescue before Jaxie could ask her why her cheeks were probably redder than Santa's coat on the keychain.

"No, you aren't dead. But you are beautiful, boss," Ron said.

Rob winked at Rachel and mouthed the words, *so are you.*

"Compliments will get you everywhere," Jaxie giggled. But she didn't leave the office as she studied Rachel with a lifted eyebrow.

Shit. Does she suspect something?

"Well, let us get out of your hair, ladies. We need to get changed before the bar opens," Ron said. He was acting as cool as a cucumber as both men moved out the open doorway. After they left, Jaxie gave a low whistle and began fanning her face with her gloved hand.

"That electric fireplace must be broke because it is steaming hot in here, girlfriend. What were the three of you doing, anyway?"

Rachel wished the floor would open up and swallow her whole. How embarrassing. How could she tell her best friend and boss that Ron and Rob were finger and mouth fucking her right here in her office while she'd been fantasizing about Santa, compliments of the keychain?

She averted Jaxie's bold gaze and picked up the Santa keychain, pretending to admire it.

"They were...just showing me the desk."

"Uh huh. Now how do I know there's more going on behind closed doors?"

Damn. Confession time. Jaxie was so going to fire her.

A sharp rap at the door made Rachel jump. Jaxie squealed with delight as a pair of knee-high, shiny leather black boots attached to a long arm suddenly protruded through the open door.

"Your boots, my lady," said a sweet feminine voice.

A woman, who Rachel remembered as the new town cobbler, walked into the room. She was petite with shoulder-length black hair. Her bright-blue eyes captured Rachel's attention. Her gaze was happy yet sad at the same time. How odd that she would think that. She didn't know anything about the woman, but she seemed to have a nice smile for her friend, Jaxie.

"Chloe, this is Rachel. Rach, Chloe," Jaxie said.

Before Rachel could say hi, Jaxie grabbed the boots and hugged them to her big belly. She was smiling so widely that Rachel thought that Jaxie had just gotten herself a fantastic deal on some sex toys.

"She's fixed my favorite old pair of leather boots! I never ever thought you could do it, Chloe."

"Hey, I'm an expert. What can I say? The boots are all fixed. Brand-new soles and I put a nice shine of mink oil on for protection. Oh! And I have orders from Ewan and Royce. Since I am heading your way, I'm to drive you home, as it is once again snowing up on the mountain and it's heading this way. They don't want you out on the roads. They said for me to tell you to leave your car in the parking lot and no arguments."

Chloe beamed and winked at Rachel. The woman gave Rachel such a warm feeling at her concern for Jaxie that for a moment Rachel wished she was Jaxie, having two great guys who really cared for her.

Before Jaxie could protest, Chloe linked her elbow with Jaxie's, waved to Rachel and then ushered Jaxie out of the office.

"See you tomorrow, Rachel!" Jaxie called out a moment later from somewhere down the hall.

"Sure thing!" Rachel called back and slumped into the new office chair, grateful that she was finally alone. Things had happened and were happening way too fast with Ron and Rob. Goodness, the things they had done to her! In here! It was mind-boggling. Nothing like that had ever happened to her.

She ogled the mini Santa that she held in her hand and felt the stirrings of excitement as she thought of Ron and Rob.

Oh boy! Oh boy! Oh boy!

They'd made her feel so good and she wanted more. So much more.

RON HAD THE HARD-ON from hell as he started to change clothes for the shift. Did Rachel not have a fucking clue how much they both were attracted to her? The cute way she'd looked up at him through thick lashes when he'd grabbed her by the elbow had instantly made him realize that up until that moment, she hadn't been aware of their feelings for her. But the hot way her dark-brown eyes flashed the instant his brother had pushed himself against her backside had just about made him come in his pants. And with everything that happened afterward...oh man!

He swore he'd jerk himself off during the first bathroom break he got tonight, because if he didn't find some relief, he'd be bending Rachel right over the bar and taking her in front of the customers.

"MAN, DID YOU SEE HOW she was reacting?" Rob chuckled a few minutes later as he met Ron in the locker room and slipped into the Key Club's traditional tight black jeans. He could barely zip himself, his erection was so big.

"I'm not sure it was only us that she was reacting to," his brother whispered as Rob donned his black muscle shirt, which had the words The Key Club scrawled across the front.

Surprise snapped through him. What was Ron saying? Surely he was joking.

"What the fuck? We were the only two guys in the office with her."

Ron looked at Rob and from the frown on his face, it didn't appear as if he were teasing him.

"Come on, why are you looking so serious?" Rob asked as uneasiness whispered through him.

"Because there was another guy in the office with us."

He almost laughed. Good one. Nice joke. Not.

But Ron continued to frown. Shit. He was kidding, wasn't he?

"You are shitting me, right? You have to be. I mean what? Someone was in the closet watching?"

"Santa was there," Ron confessed.

Fucking asshole. Within a split second, Rob picked up a nearby towel and flicked it at his brother's left hip. Ron let out a yelp of pain and moved away from him.

Good. That serves him for acting like an idiot. Santa. Geez.

"Stop fucking around, man. She was reacting to us, not some keychain."

"She was staring at Santa while we were arousing her. She was getting off on all three of us."

His brother didn't so much as crack a grin. Was Ron serious?

"That's why she reacted at the mention of the Santa Ménage Night. She *seriously* does have a Santa fetish. Jaxie must know about it, and that's why she's throwing one for her. And I have to admit, instead of being turned off that she has a Santa fetish, it turns me on. Big time," Ron admitted.

"I guess we have a way now of getting to know her as intimately as two men can know a woman, outside of what just happened with her," his brother said softly.

Rob nodded. It appeared that they did.

He enjoyed the look of understanding in Ron's eyes. His brother knew all about the world of fetishes. Hell, their fetish was sharing a woman. They both got off watching the other pleasure a woman they both liked. Since meeting Rachel, no other woman had captured their attention in the interest department.

They needed to explore this sizzling attraction and if they had to do it with the help of the jolly old Saint Nick, then so be it.

RACHEL STARED OUT OF her living room window and watched the lacy swirls of snowflakes spiral out of the late evening sky. Disappointment rocked her. Weather reports warned of an approaching snowstorm, and Jaxie was hinting at possibly closing the club for the Santa Fetish Ménage Night festivities. Jaxie had said she didn't want to be responsible for her patrons getting into accidents on icy roads. But the final decision wouldn't come until the day before and that meant she would be on pins and needles until tomorrow.

Man, this situation with Rob and Ron sucked. Rachel still couldn't believe what had gone on in her new office the other day. Since then, the guys had sent her heated looks that had her on the edge expecting them to bust into her office any minute and give her another round of pleasure...or other naughty things that shouldn't be happening at the workplace. But nothing had happened. The few times she'd been forced to chat with Ron or Rob, the incident hadn't been mentioned and they'd both acted all business like.

Had she been reading too much into what had happened? Had she been their play toy? Or had they realized they just weren't into her?

Rachel frowned at that last thought. The idea that she'd been wrong about them being interested in her shot shards of sadness into her. Why couldn't she be lucky like Jaxie? She loved Jaxie like her own sister, but sometimes Rachel wished she could be like her. Was that evil to think something like this about her friend?

Jaxie had admitted to having sex with Ewan in her office. It was how she'd conceived the baby. Unprotected office sex.

Jaxie and Ewan had been apart for months. Rachel had arranged it so Ewan would find her in her office one night by pretending Jaxie had left behind a cell phone at Ewan's workplace — a search and rescue unit located on a mountain peak just outside of town.

Ewan had been kind to return the cell phone to Jaxie. Apparently, they'd fought, and then had hate sex or maybe make-up sex. Not too long after, Jaxie and Ewan had reunited during a Ménage night with Ewan's good friend, Royce.

Now the three of them lived together in the house across the street. Wanting to have two guys for her very own, was a secret Rachel had carried around with her ever since she'd heard about Jaxie creating the Key Club and matchmaking threesomes.

Rachel frowned. But that would never happen to her. She was way too embarrassed to let Rob and Ron know about her Santa fetish even with the two of them expressing an interest in her.

Both of them.

Would she have reacted so strongly to what they'd done to her had she not already been aroused looking at those fetish toys earlier during the business meeting? Or had having that Santa right there in front of her when they'd been touching her so intimately set her off in such a wild way?

Rachel drew her gaze from the falling snow and to the adorable Santa keychain the guys had given her. She'd placed the white-bearded stuffed man on the coffee table when she'd come home and now, as she looked at it, the naughty stirrings of excitement whispered through her.

Gosh, their intimate touches had just about drove her wild. The searing way Rob's fingers had plunged in and out of her pussy like a miniature cock out of control, had quickly brought her to orgasm. Not to mention Ron's tongue lashing her nipples into pert, attention-seeking traitors. She needed his mouth on her breasts again. Wanted Rob sucking her clit again. Wanted them both of them in her bed, thrusting into her, making love to her. But she could never tell them about Santa.

It was...embarrassing.

Rachel inhaled deeply and tried to steady her quickening breaths. She jumped as the phone suddenly rang. A quick look at her call display, and she noted Jaxie was calling. For a second she thought about letting it go to voice mail. She didn't want to listen to bad news about the party being cancelled.

But her anticipation won out and she picked up the receiver. She just needed to keep calm, no matter what Jaxie had decided.

"Hey Jax, how's it going?"

"Hiya Rachel. I've been thinking about tomorrow night."

Rachel's tummy dipped at the solemn sound of her friend's voice. Shoot! She was going to cancel the themed night.

"The storm is going to be bad," Jaxie said.

Rachel's hopes plummeted. *This sucks*!

"But not as bad as they are predicting."

What? Was that a yes? She held her breath as her anticipation soared.

"So, we're going to open. But I need you to run the place tomorrow night. Ewan and Royce are refusing to let me leave the house because of the storm. Can you believe those two? They're so sweet."

What? No!

"They keep badgering me to slow down, as it's way too close to my due date. They want me off my feet from here on out," Jaxie chuckled lightly, but Rachel didn't quite hear what Jaxie was saying, as an idea of how she could go to the party began to dance in her head.

"And you know me, I just can't argue with the guys," Jaxie continued.

A sudden bout of guilt smacked her. Oh, she had to stop this! Jaxie was number one now and Rachel had come back to help her out. She needed to stop putting herself before Jaxie.

"No problem, Jax. You can count on me," she replied. But it was so hard to keep the disappointment out of her voice and to share in Jaxie's happiness.

"Thanks, sweetie. You are a doll."

"That's what you pay me the big bucks for." She wanted to say thanks again to Jaxie about her new office, but she kept quiet. She didn't want to bring up any questions about the office that she didn't wish to answer.

Suddenly, she heard one of the guys — she wasn't sure which one — curse while Jaxie was speaking.

Concern rippled over her. "Is everything okay, Jax?"

Jaxie laughed. "It's Royce. He's making us dinner tonight. He just dropped a fork on his big toe," Jaxie's voice grew muffled. "Don't worry, babe, I'll kiss it and make it all better."

Rachel giggled. Jaxie was so comfortable with her men.

"Sorry, Rach. I gotta go. Thanks again. I really appreciate it."

Before Rachel could say goodbye, the line went dead.

Wow. She would not mind having a man cook for her, let alone two men insisting she not work.

Yeah, she could get used to having a couple of hotties around here in her house and keeping her safe and snug while a winter storm blasted away outdoors. But she'd never get that lucky. The only luck that was in store for her was trying to figure out how to get to Santa Fetish Ménage Night without anyone knowing it was her.

Rachel sighed and hung up the phone.

Chapter Four

"SO...HAVE YOU FOUND what you are looking for...um, for your friend?" Jewel said as she entered the deserted dressing room hallway where Rachel stood in front of the full-length mirror.

Jewel stood behind Rachel and smiled at her in the mirror.

Rachel nodded. Yeah, this was the one. This was the one she wanted to wear to the gala. She'd figured everything out and come hell or high water, she was going to get two Santas for one pleasure-filled night at the Key Club. And this sexy Santa Baby spaghetti-strap dress with white marabou trim, lace-up front and black lace glovettes was going to go perfect with the thigh-high black leather boots she'd bought while in Paris.

As Jewel caught her gaze in the mirror, Rachel cursed silently as her cheeks warmed and grew rosy. She hated lying to Jewel, but she just wasn't ready to reveal her fetish.

"I think my friend is going to be pleased," Rachel answered.

Jewel smiled. "Good. You are a dear for keeping your friend's secret. And I should add that outfit also comes with black glovettes and something special."

To Rachel's surprise, Jewel brought out a Santa Claus cupcake in the palm of her hand. "Made the cupcakes myself," Jewel said with pride sparkling in her eyes.

Rachel stared down at the swirls of red, white and black icing made out to look exactly like Santa.

"Wow! That Santa looks hot!"

Jewel laughed. "Hot? I've never had a compliment like that before. Anyway, I will pack a couple with the outfit...if you want it?"

"This is what I...I mean it's perfect for her."

Jewel's eyes twinkled. "You make sure you give your friend a cupcake and save the other for yourself. Okay?"

Rachel grinned. Oh, she'd be indulging on Santa. She loved cupcakes. Too bad cupcakes didn't like her waistline or she'd indulge every day. But since this was Christmas holiday time...

She hurried to undress. So far, her plan was coming along without a hitch. Now she had one more stop to make, and if all went well, she'd be on her merry way to the Key Club's Santa Fetish Ménage Night.

THIS IS SURREAL, Rachel thought as she huddled deeper into the red coat with the white fur-lined hem and hood that she'd also purchased from Jewel. She'd been waiting anxiously in her car in the parking lot for a lull in the traffic. Despite the warning of the snowstorm, it looked like a good turnout tonight. Now that the parking lot was finally empty of people, she quickly dashed out of her snow-covered car, locked it and walked toward the Club.

At the front steps, Rachel stopped and took a few steadying breaths. Through the swirling snow, she stared at the handmade Santa logs adorning each step. Each log was about three feet tall, and split in the middle. Each split half was painted like Santa. So cute. She'd put Ron and Rob in charge of the decorations because they'd practically begged her for the job.

Now she understood why they'd volunteered. They actually knew what they were doing.

Tiny pale-red and black fairy lights glistened in the frost-encrusted windows of the Club and as she ascended the stairs, a large Santa hat laden with red silk poinsettias hung on the front door.

Rachel's pulse picked up speed and she inhaled sharply as she pushed open the door and stepped into the building. There was a large crowd of red, white and black. Everywhere. Everyone was dressed as Santa, Sexy Santa or Mrs. Claus.

Rachel smiled. She'd blend in perfectly.

Earlier today, she'd asked Sophie, the town hairstylist and her friend, as well as her once part-time employer, to give her a new look. Thankfully, Sophie had kept curious questions at bay. She'd come through for her, dying Rachel's hair a pretty blonde. Sophie had also tweaked Rachel's eyebrows and given her makeup tips to change her appearance.

All Rachel needed to do now was melt into the shadows and maybe get some dancing in, grab some drinks and get excited in the sea of Santas. She checked her coat at the coat check pretending to be busy on her cell, keeping her face averted to the young woman, a pre-med student. *What is her name? Ah yes, Charley.*

Jaxie had recently hired Charley to work at the Key Club, and Rachel didn't want Charley to recognize her. The woman stamped Rachel's hand with her coat number and then Rachel quickly lost herself in the Santa theme settling herself at a secluded table for two along a far wall.

Yep, the guys had outdone themselves with the decorations inside as well. The place looked spectacular.

Red-and-white Santa hat chair covers embraced every chair. Each table was covered in a sparkling white linen with a large, foot-high pine cone Christmas tree set in a miniature terra cotta pot placed in the center of each table. Each pine cone was painted green, and the tips of the cone petals had been painted white to give a snow-frosted appearance. Tiny Christmas lights of blue, green, yellow and red, adorned each pine cone.

Everything looked so pretty. It was as if Rachel had left reality and been thrust into a world of...well, a magical world of Santa. Excitement spun through her as she gazed at the Santa belt napkin rings adorning dark-green napkins at each place setting.

Simple. Elegant. Perfect.

The music was a wild Christmas tempo and in the background she heard something that made her blood boil in a really nice way.

"Ho! Ho! Ho!" came a guttural voice from a nearby corner.

The sound sent exquisite shivers along her flesh. Suddenly the crowd parted giving her a glimpse of Santa seated on a chair right beside a gorgeous live eight-foot-high blue-Scotch pine Christmas tree.

"Ho! Ho! Ho!" Santa shouted.

Gosh, she liked the way her skin tingled as he shouted. Rachel watched as a woman dressed as Mrs. Claus sat down on his knee and he gave her a large red lollipop.

She'd love to be in that woman's place...Rachel blew out a long breath.

"Would you like to order a drink?" A woman asked a couple that sat right beside Rachel.

Shit! She recognized Ava, the woman Rachel had asked to take over for her tonight. Jaxie had hired Ava to help out at the Key Club while Rachel had been in Europe.

Man, she did not want Ava to recognize her, so she pulled her Santa hat lower over her forehead. She flipped open her cell phone, grabbed her notebook from her purse and plopped it onto the table, grabbed her pen and scribbled her order. When Ava moved to her table, Rachel made sure to keep her face averted and held up her notebook with the drink written on the page.

"Vanilla Peppermint Martini, double double. Coming right up," Ava said and then she drifted away into the crowd.

Rachel sighed with relief.

Boy, that was close.

Placing her cell back onto the table, Rachel checked out the bar area. Rob and Ron would be working tonight, both dressed as Santa. Sure enough, there were two Santas there. She really should go over and thank them for their awesome decorations.

But she couldn't. Her secret fetish would be revealed.

Rachel frowned. It sucked keeping a low profile while everyone else was out in the open, their fetishes accepted by the crowd. There were so many times she wished she wasn't ashamed for being sexually aroused by Santa.

Rachel tensed as she spied Ava approaching with her drink.

Rachel grabbed her cell and pretended to be listening.

"Your drink, my dear. Compliment of the gentlemen at the bar."

Men at the bar? Shit! Was someone hitting on her already?

Ava didn't wait for her to answer, and quickly disappeared into the crowd again. Rachel gazed at the bar area. It was lined with a row of red, white and black Santas and sexy Santas. No one was paying her any attention. Who in the world had sent her the drink?

Rachel removed the red-and-white striped candy cane and the mint sprig from the liquid and grabbed her glass. It was cold and the glass sparkled with dew, the rim dusted with crushed candy cane. The scent of peppermint and vanilla made Rachel's mouth water. She lifted the glass but then hesitated as something on her table caught her eye.

Ava had left a napkin. She froze as she realized someone had written on it in black bold handwriting.

Rachel,

For a lovely, relaxing and Santa-filled evening, you have come to the right place. We want you exactly the way you are. We are extending an invitation to join us in the Red Room. If you do accept our invitation, the safe word is RED.

P.S. Don't bring your sexy clothes

Your two hot Santas.

Two hot Santas? We want you just the way you are? Rachel rolled her eyes and cursed silently beneath her breath.

Come on. Had someone already recognized her? How was that even possible? Even she hadn't recognized herself when she'd put on her makeup and gazed in the mirror.

She narrowed her gaze as she spied something sticking out from beneath the napkin. She lifted the napkin and gasped. It was a gorgeous red skeleton key with a Santa head complete with hat, white beard and ruby-red cheeks.

Someone knew it was her? Someone must have planned all this? She hadn't been here more than ten minutes. Unless she was just being targeted at random?

Rachel hadn't told anyone she was coming here. Not even Jewel. Unless Jewel had guessed the dress Rachel had purchased was actually for her and not a friend, like she'd told Jewel?

What in the world should she do?

Leave? Or pretend she'd not seen the note and just go in and pick a ménage key and have sex with Santa strangers?

She stared at the note. *Someone wants me just the way I am?*

Should she accept the invitation?

Us. The note said us. Ménage.

Santa-filled evening.

For a moment, Rachel wanted to cry. Was her secret out? How could she ever face anyone again? This was so not the way she wanted things to happen tonight. So. Not.

She stared at the note again.

If you accept the invitation. Red Room. Safe word. Red.

When a safe word was involved, that meant some form of bondage. Santa tying her up, or tying her down, or both? Maybe some pleasure-pain?

Rachel took a sip of her drink. The refreshing mint schnapps, vodka and lime in the drink burst over her taste buds along with the sweetness of the candy cane on the rim.

Oh darn, what in the world should she do?

Hmm, Rachel seemed a bit rattled by that note. But she'd recovered quickly. A glance toward the bar to see who was watching, then back to the note again.

Good. The longer she took to decide, the more in their favor. If Rachel accepted the invitation, then all the worrying had been for naught. Rachel's happiness was all they wanted.

She'd been through so much with her dad, and she deserved some happiness. Now all she needed to do was go to the Red Room.

Come on, Rachel. Follow your instincts and leave the rest to us.

Instincts told her that someone was watching her. But who? Rachel kept scanning the crowd but everyone appeared to be in their own Santa world.

"Ho! Ho! Ho!" Santa cheered, making her naughty side emerge again.

Casually she continued to sip her drink and perused the dance floor, the bar and dark alcoves. No one paid her any mind. She was just a wallflower. Nothing wrong with that. She was never one for being the center of attention.

It was another reason why she'd made it her business to keep quiet about her fetish. Yet now, someone knew. Despite that, her world had not fallen apart. Whoever had written that note was embracing her, despite her fetish. They'd gone out of their way for her in writing the note, and inviting her to the Red Room.

Rachel smiled as she finished her drink.

She knew what to do.

RACHEL'S HANDS TREMBLED as half an hour later, she twisted the key in the lock and let herself into the Red Room. She'd freshened up by taking a shower. She'd left her clothing in a locker, grabbed one of the freshly scented terrycloth robes available to Key Club members and put it on. The softness of the robe embraced her and made her a little less nervous. Thankfully, there had been no women in the locker room to witness her nervousness or to identify her. They were all waiting to be able to pick the key that would lead them to the respective rooms where they would meet their two guys. Just as she was doing now.

Which two guys would be for her? Who knew about her fetish?

Curiosity urged her to step into the Red Room.

The first thing she saw when she cleared the small hallway was a cute live blue spruce Christmas tree. Her breath caught as she gazed at the red bows and bright-red lights draped on the branches, along with the array of Santa Claus ornaments decorating the tree. At the tip of the tree stood a gorgeous two-foot high Santa.

There was a huge bed near the tree. The comforter was a Santa Claus bedcover and the pillows were red with white snowflakes. Gray lamps with blue shades were set on each side of the bed on nightstands.

Winter-themed paintings and photos hung on the walls, and it was as if she'd been plopped into Santa's very own bedroom. It was something right out of her own dreams.

As Rachel peered out the second-floor windows, she noticed the spiralling snowflakes. It was a virtual white blanket descending and she couldn't even see the towering pine trees that lined the property of the Key Club. Wind whipped against the frosted windowpanes, emitting a spooky howling sound. Outside it looked ugly and nasty. She blew out a tense breath.

Inside, it was just wonderful. Warmth filled her as she gazed at the modern white marble electric fireplace. Yellow flames licked orange coals and imitation logs, and the fire tossed a friendly glow over everything. Three over-filled red stockings hung from the mantel. Green garland laden with red bows and red berries was strewn across the top of the mantel and a huge wooden heart with the words Merry Christmas carved into it hung over the fireplace.

Rachel was about to explore what was inside the stockings when as she passed the large bed, she spied a red sheet of paper, and several red ropes with small golden bells attached to the ends were lying on one of the pillows.

She picked up the paper and her heart fluttered with excitement.

Get naked and put on the restraints. Because your Santas are coming to town...for you. Ring the jingle bells when you're ready.

Rachel's legs trembled as she removed her robe and hung it on a nearby hook. She slipped off the throwaway slippers supplied by The Key Club and slid them beneath the bed. The ultra-soft mattress dipped as she crawled onto the bed and sat in the middle. She placed a sheet over herself and then gazed at the ankle and wrist restraints. She could smell the leather of the black cuffs and noted the insides were fur-lined for comfort. Each cuff was attached to its own gold chain, which disappeared behind the sides of the bed.

Rachel bit her bottom lip as she snapped the cuffs around each of her ankles and noted the chains gave her no choice but to be spread-eagled. Then, with trembling fingers, she snapped on one of her wrist cuffs, then lay down. She stared up at the mirrored ceiling and inhaled a shaky breath.

She looked...different with blonde hair and makeup instead of her normal mousy-brown hair and a trace of blush and lipstick. Not quite herself. But that was okay. She certainly felt herself, giddy with excitement and nerves as she gazed around the room at the items she hadn't noticed when she'd first come in. She'd been in this room many times for other ménage nights, but as an employee, not as a customer. Winter-themed paintings and photos had been suspended on the walls. The stockings had been hung by the fireplace with care and it was so quiet, not a creature was stirring not even a mouse.

Rachel chuckled out loud at her train of thoughts. It was Christmastime and the first holiday without her father. Sadness struck her and tears welled in her eyes.

She gave her head a firm shake. No. She'd grieved enough for now. She wanted to be happy tonight. She wanted to be daring and naughty. All the things she'd put off while caring for her dad.

Pushing aside her sad thoughts, Rachel gazed around the room and focused on more of the details. Red and green votive candles flickered on a nearby wood shelf and the delicate scent of fresh pine drifted through the air. Dainty white Styrofoam snowflakes dangled from tiny hooks in the ceiling, giving a snow effect. There were even several boughs of mistletoe interspersed with the snowflakes.

Rachel smiled. Whoever had decorated this room had a flair for romance.

But who had invited her here?

Again that inner nervousness of someone knowing about her fetish scrambled through her. She pushed it aside. She'd deceived many people so she could make her secret dream come true tonight. By gosh, she was going to enjoy it!

Rachel peeked past the foot of her bed and caught sight of a metal cart pushed into a dark corner. Usually, the carts were filled with an assortment of naughty toys. When she stocked the carts, she took great joy imaging the excitement customers felt when they found them.

She frowned. This cart had no toys for her.

She shook her head and emitted a sharp sigh. She was being silly. She didn't need toys, she just needed a couple of hot Santas screwing her brains out. She chuckled at that thought, reached out and grabbed the ropes with the bells.

Here I go. She held her breath, gave the ropes a tentative shake and jumped at the loud jingles.

Goodness, the entire club could hear. The Santas would think her desperate. She dropped the rope with bells and her nervousness edged up.

She didn't have too long to wait, as not even a minute later, a key rattled in the door.

They're here.

Chapter Five

RACHEL'S HEART POUNDED with a maddening speed as two men dressed in Santa suits entered the room. They weren't chubby like the Clauses she'd seen by the Christmas tree downstairs. But they did have full white beards and the red-and-white suits and hats.

Heat and pleasure flooded her.

They looked...perfect.

She stared at them, her mouth dropping in awe as one Santa strolled up beside the bed and looked down at her. His eyes twinkled cheerily as he latched her remaining wrist restraint.

Who are you? With the white beards, curling mustaches, white hair and their Santa hats pulled low over their foreheads, she couldn't tell. But they smelled so nice. Just like...

Rachel tensed as she suddenly recognized their odors.

No. Way. Could it be...?

The Santa who'd just done up the last restraint sat down on the bed.

"You looked so damned sexy when you walked into the building, Rachel."

That voice. Rob? Or was it Ron? She couldn't tell which one.

Oh, no. No. No.

How in the world did *they* know?

Her face flamed. She pulled on her restraints. Shit. Tight. Captive.

"We wanted to take you right then and there. Right up against the front door," Ron said. Yes, it had to be Ron. Or Rob?

Take me up against the door?

Wow, that would be incredibly sexy.

"We would have, too, had there not been an audience," the other Santa said. He stood beside the fireplace and gazed at the red stockings.

She wasn't used to this kind of talk. Talk from two men who wanted her so badly that they'd set up this room for her?

Shoot, Rachel was still reeling from what had happened to her in her office with these two. She should have known something was up when they'd suddenly acted like perfect employees after that episode in her new office.

The Santa who'd been gazing at the stockings began picking them off their respective hooks. With his arms laden, he moved to a metal cart, placed the plump stockings onto the cart and wheeled it over to beside the bed.

She wanted to tell Rob and Ron this was all some weird misunderstanding, but her thoughts died as the Santa sitting on the bed beside her lifted one of the stockings from the car and dumped the contents onto the bed.

Wow, there were an abundance of colorful Christmas-flavored condoms. Brown cinnamon, green-and-white striped peppermint, and red cranberry. Exactly how long were they planning on keeping her here?

Rachel whimpered involuntarily at the thought of being tied to the bed while the Santas took turns pleasuring her through the night.

She watched them as they each picked up a stocking and dumped their contents beside the pile of condoms. Toys spilled out over the sheets. A red Santa-themed vibrator, black cock rings for the guys, and...Oh boy. It was getting way too hot in here.

The two Santas drew their attention from the pile of toys back to her. She trembled as their hot gazes moved hungrily over her sheet-covered body. She dared to gaze down to investigate what had piqued their interest and inhaled sharply at how her nipples boldly poked against the sheets.

"What's the safe word?" The Santa closest to her asked. His voice was serious, but with an undertow of a gentleness.

"Red," she whispered.

"Don't be afraid to use it if you need to. You belong to us, no matter what," the other Santa said. It was then that she finally figured out which Santa was Rob and which was Ron. She remembered Rob's voice could be commanding and Ron's voice just as forceful also, but with a gentler edge. Knowing who was who now made her relax. If only a little.

Lordy. This is not happening.

It was like stuff out of her naughtiest fantasy dreams. Even better, because this was reality.

Both of them continued to stare at her, their eyes glistening with hunger. Her senses reeled as she tried to make sense of everything.

"You really have no idea how much we want you, do you, Rachel?" Ron's question torpedoed into her. Automatically, she shook her head.

Both men swore softly.

Dear me. They *really* were serious.

"We'll have to show you," Rob growled as he slipped his fingers beneath the top of the sheet covering her. Without hesitation, he snapped the sheet from her body.

Warm air breathed against her naked flesh and her inner thighs clenched at the appreciation twinkling her Santas' eyes.

"You've been very naughty, Rachel. Very naughty for not realizing how much we want you in our life," Rob whispered.

He pulled off his white beard and placed it on the bed near the pile of toys. His lips were red and lush and she ached to have him kissing her.

Disbelief melted into her. She'd come here expecting a couple of Santas to pleasure her, but knowing it was Ron and Rob, her reaction to what was happening was more intense than she expected. She didn't know what to think. Didn't know *how* to think.

"Santa is extremely disappointed in naughty girls," Ron said softly as he lifted a large red-and-white striped candy-cane-colored double vibrator.

"But you can redeem yourself in Santa's eyes, Rachel baby," Rob added.

She held her breath as Rob began undressing. The buckle clinked as he undid it, then he slipped off his belt and dropped it to the floor. She watched, her body tense with anticipation, as the Ron liberally smeared lube on the vibe.

Movement caught her gaze, and Rachel looked to catch Rob drop his red pants. He wore nothing but a very large erection. It angled up toward his abdomen, and to her amusement, his shaft appeared to have been painted as a Santa, complete with red Santa hat, white beard and black beady eyes.

She laughed.

"You like?" Rob asked with a chuckle. His Santa cock gently bobbed as he moved onto the bed and climbed over her to quickly position his pelvis over her face. She stared at the Santa cock and felt the familiar stirrings of arousal swiftly build. She also caught the scent of mint drifting off his flesh and suddenly realized he wasn't climbing over her just to show off his cock's new look.

Her eyes widened. He wanted her to...

He must have noticed her reaction for he stopped, his cock poised a few inches from her face.

"Have you ever taken a man orally before, Rachel?" he asked. His voice was strained and she suspected he knew the answer already.

She thought about lying, but then instead she shook her head.

Both men swore softly.

For a moment, embarrassment flushed through her. She was in her late twenties with virtually no sexual experience. Everyone she knew had been having sex for years but she'd been too busy to experiment.

"Don't be shy, baby. I'll be gentle...for now," Rob growled. "Open your mouth, sweetness, Open your mouth to Santa, he needs you so bad."

Rachel trembled as the white fur from his red Santa jacket caressed her forehead. She did his bidding, opening her mouth and his Santa shaft came closer. The succulent scent of mint grew.

She closed her eyes and moaned as he moved the hot smooth tip of his shaft over her lips, circling them as if it were a tube of lipstick.

Her lips tingled wherever he touched and she melted into the wonderful sensations.

"You like that, huh, baby," he groaned. His voice was thick and aroused. His cock jerked against her lips.

She stuck out her tongue and took a tentative lick of his smooth cockhead. Peppermint *and* chocolate splashed over her taste buds. He growled. The animalistic sound pounded through her like an aphrodisiac. She wanted to hear more.

"You taste good," she whispered. She loved how her lips tingled. Enjoyed the cool chocolate flavor enveloping her mouth.

"It's edible body paint. Comes in different colors. It's called 'Make-Me-Hot Chocolate Mint' sensual enhancer," he said with a chuckle.

He pressed his shaft against her mouth and she opened to him. He slid in a couple of inches and she tightened her lips around his shaft.

"That's it, start sucking. Nice and slow. You've got precious cargo in your mouth. No biting."

Rachel smiled around his shaft. He had to mention biting, didn't he? Now she suddenly had the urge to tease him with a few subtle nips. Using her tongue, she stroked his hard flesh and then sucked alternately, allowing her teeth to delicately run along the length of his cock as he withdrew.

He moaned and swore softly. It appeared he enjoyed her teeth. She continued doing what she was doing and listened to how his breaths came faster and raspier.

Surprise rocked her as the mattress between her legs moved.

Ron.

"Relax, baby. He's just going to prepare you for us."

I'm already prepared, she wanted to say as a demanding rush for pleasure raced through her. Before she could speak, a slippery, thick object pressed gently into her vagina. It had to be the dual vibrator she'd seen Ron pick up earlier.

"Just concentrate on what you're doing, sweetness. Santa will take good care of you," Rob said in a strangled voice from just above her.

Sure, easy for you to say. You don't have a cock in your mouth and a double vibe coming in between your legs.

She kept up her ministrations on Rob's jerking erection.

The head of the vibe was smooth and warm, and the pressure of it stretched past her pussy muscles. Rachel fought to remain calm as the other shaft on the vibe pressed against her tight sphincter. It burned and pushed, pleasure-pain sparking along her nerves as the toy penetrated her ass. Fiery heat quickly fanned through her ass as the intruders vibrated and heated.

Both shafts were heavily lubed as they stretched into her, causing her muscles to clench around them. A moment later a stimulator trembled against her clitoris, sending wicked sensations of pleasure into her. She cried out and involuntarily gyrated her hips.

"Good girl," Ron whispered. "That's it, take it in."

She moaned against the thick invasions and kept sucking on Rob's cock while Ron pushed the toy deeper.

Ron withdrew and then thrust the dual vibrator into her again. Her senses spun as he teased her with a few short thrusts and she moaned as he impaled her fully, the stimulator eagerly massaging her clit.

Rob began thrusting into her mouth. His groans grew louder as she tightened her suction. She liked the raspy sound of his breaths as she caressed his steel-hard flesh with her tongue. Blood pumped through her and she clenched her fists and pulled against her restraints as arousal spiralled through her.

Ron's deep and fast thrusts of the vibe whipped tremors of need through her and warm liquid gushed down her channel.

"She's creaming beautifully, Santa," Ron said in a hoarse voice.

Rob answered with an erotic grunt. His pistoning grew frantic and his cock was jerking against her tingling lips as he slid in and out like a piston.

"Too...damned...good," Rob growled. "Can't...stop."

Ron chuckled. Untamed thrills at his laughter whipped through her.

She sucked Rob harder. Between her thighs, Ron's thrusts grew faster, deeper.

Her clit throbbed as the massager pummeled her sensitive flesh. Her vagina and ass were filled to perfection.

Without warning, an explosion sent shockwaves through her. Rachel lost control and dove into the pleasure. It wrapped around her, kissed her, and loved her. It sunk so deep she swore it penetrated her bones, making her legs quiver and her body shudder uncontrollably.

Ron withdrew the toy and Rachel bucked and cried out as his hot, firm mouth melted over her pussy. His tongue circled her tender clit, snapping another round of arousal through her. She creamed and Ron sucked her arousal from her body.

The heat of his mouth, and the licks of his tongue shattered her mind. She thought nothing. Felt everything.

Heat, pleasure, tremors and a need to be wanted by them.

Gosh! It was so intense. Too wild. She'd never felt so out of control before. She was going to lose her mind. Lose herself in this pleasure. If she wasn't careful, they would become addictive. *Oh hell, who am I kidding? They are addictive.*

They kept her on the edge and then pushed her over several times, making her shudder and convulse as pleasure waves lashed her. Abruptly, Rob warned her that he was coming. Hot spurts swept into her mouth and she fought to swallow. Instincts took over and she calmed herself and accepted his seed. By the time Rob was finished and he'd withdrawn, she smiled.

Gosh, she felt like a freaking pro already. But there was a sharp painful need building. She wanted more from them. So much more than just sex.

Pleasure raced through Ron as he watched Rachel. Her fists were clenched and the soles of her feet were pressed into the mattress as she twisted against her restraints while he'd made her come over and over again with the toy. His penis was killing him. It jerked against the restriction of his Santa trousers as he'd watched his brother fucking her perfect mouth and listened to her sweet tortured whimpers. He wanted nothing more than to position himself over her sweet, writhing body, kiss her senseless and bury his aching cock deep inside of her warm, tight pussy.

He'd never experienced such an intense attraction to a woman before. Having her here, splayed out and at their mercy, warmed his heart and had him visibly shaking from the need to make her belong to him. To them.

Hell, he'd never had sex in a workplace before either, and yet here he was at the Key Club pleasuring a woman he and his brother both wanted.

Having her here in one of the Key Club rooms was a fantasy come to life. With her admitting she was inexperienced in the sex department, it made his attraction to her increase to such a degree it just about killed him.

He struggled to draw air into his lungs. He was breathing way too fast as he'd sucked the cream from her convulsing pussy. She tasted so beautiful. Everything about her was flawless. She was a dream come to life.

She was *his*.

Rob hadn't been able to get enough of her. She'd sucked him so sweetly, so innocently that it was a wonder he hadn't come before he did. He'd wanted to, many times, but he'd barely managed the thin thread of self-control as she'd whimpered her arousal.

Whatever Ron had been doing to her with that vibrator, she enjoyed it. He hadn't wanted to stop listening to her erotic sounds and he'd loved the intense way her mouth tightened around his flesh every time she came.

But the storm building inside him had finally come to a head and he'd exploded. Bright lights had burst behind his eyes as his shaft pulsed and jerked against her hot lips. He'd been surprised she'd been able to handle what he'd done to her. That she'd been so eager to please, especially with what Ron had been doing to her while Rob had been fucking her.

He grinned as he climbed off her. She was a quick learner. He liked that. Liked that a lot.

Chapter Six

"LET'S TAKE A BREAK, babe," Ron whispered against Rachel's ear. She forced herself to open her eyes. Had she fallen asleep? Or had she fallen into a sex-induced trance after her last orgasm? She couldn't remember. Nor could she remember being released from her binds and being covered by a nice cozy Santa Claus comforter.

Before she could even gather some thoughts, one of Ron's hands slid beneath her thighs and another slid beneath her upper back. Suddenly, she was airborne as he lifted her.

"Where are we going?" she asked, unsure of what was happening.

"We're going to take a nice warm shower to wash away all your aches," Ron said softly. To her surprise, his warm lips brushed gently against her mouth. Her lips quivered in response. And then she tasted mint.

Mmm, he kissed nice. Really nice.

"I don't ache. I want to be fucked."

Mercy! Had she just said that out loud?

"That can easily be arranged, baby," Ron muttered and gave her mouth another brush with his teasing lips.

"More kisses," she whispered. Was this really happening? Was she so easily influenced emotionally by a kiss? Why was she being so bold? She'd never been this bold with a guy before.

"Refreshments first," Rob suddenly said as Ron carried her into the adjoining bathroom.

Jaxie had outdone herself with all the Key Club bathrooms. They were very roomy. Some had Jacuzzis, or small pools, and this one had a state-of-the-art shower as well as an adjoining lounge area, where Ron was now carrying her too.

The room had been decorated in a Santa theme in here as well. Santa hat shower curtain hooks held a Santa-themed shower curtain. Pretty red fairy lights had been strewn over the large bathroom mirror. The towels were red and black, and the immediate floor area was covered by a large Santa rug. It all looked so lovely.

Ron set her down on a warm, padded red lounge chair and readjusted the comforter around her so her arms were free and the rest of her was covered. He'd draped her most likely due to her inexperience. But that was okay, because a sudden bout of shyness was gripping her now. Especially after what had just happened between the three of them had begun to sink into her quickly formulating thoughts.

Rachel just couldn't believe she'd been so wanton and naked in front of her co-workers. Not to mention being tied down and having two guys pleasuring her. It was wicked. It was wild. It was something she wanted to do again. And again.

Her cheeks suddenly flamed.

"Here you go, sweetheart. This champagne will cool you down. You look flushed," Rob said as he handed her a long-stemmed flute.

She nodded her thanks and quickly sipped it, loving the cool, soft splash against her tongue and taste buds.

The two men wheeled a cart laden with Santa-themed food beside her and began piling food onto a plate. She grinned as she eyed the Santa-hat brownies, Santa strawberries – strawberries filled with whipped cream and chocolate sprinkles as eyes — strands of red grapes impaled on Santa-themed toothpicks, reindeer cookies, and even slices of kiwi fruit made to look like a Christmas tree.

The abundance of color looked so pretty that it brought tears to Rachel's eyes. She quickly brushed them away with the back of her hand.

"Geez, I think we made her cry," Rob said as he quickly passed Rachel a dark-green napkin.

"No, it's just...I'm overwhelmed," she admitted. "You've done so much for me and I don't know why."

Both men looked stricken, and then Rachel remembered their earlier conversation when they'd asked her if she truly didn't understand how much they cared for her.

"There's something about you, Rachel," Ron said as she sat down on the lounge beside her and held out a plate laden with the delightful-looking treats.

"Yeah, we sensed it right from the minute we met you. You are the one for us," Rob said quickly.

Oh.

While she'd drifted into that sex stupor or whatever it had been, Rob had put his red Santa pants on and she noticed the area between his thighs was tented.

Goodness, did she really turn him on this much?

"You're so sweet and innocent. We like that in a woman," Ron assured her and nodded to the plate.

"Take some nourishment. We aren't finished with you. Not by far."

This is nuts. But she loved their attentiveness. So this must be what Jaxie experienced with her two guys. And the other friends who were in ménage relationships.

In awe. Grateful to have their attention and their caring.

It was as if she was being embraced in a cotton falls of...protectiveness and love.

Rachel picked a strawberry and took a bite. Sweet juice mingled with the sugary whipped cream and she couldn't stop moaning at how incredibly delicious it tasted.

"Baby, you'd better tone that cute sound down, or we'll be fucking you right here and now," Ron warned.

Both men stared at her with intent in their heated gazes. Fire flamed through her at their meaning.

Rachel rubbed the cold champagne glass against her flaming cheeks, careful not to spill the contents. She wanted to tell them to go right ahead, but her shyness prevented her. Gosh, she really needed to work on that.

"I have a question," she said to change the subject.

"Ask us anything, sweet princess. We are slaves of your heart," Rob said with a wink. He tossed a brownie into his mouth and chewed slowly, seductively, and she imagined him going down on her.

Lordy, she needed to get her bearings! She took a few gulps of the champagne for courage. The buzz came quickly, as she wasn't one for drinking.

"How...how did you know? About my um...liking Santa?" For some reason she just couldn't say the word fetish.

She didn't miss the odd look that passed between the two men. Okay, instincts told her that they had a secret.

"Well...you came here. We saw you and we made the invitation," Ron said carefully.

Rachel shook her head. "Not buying it."

"Have some more food," Ron replied and held up the plate again.

"Stalling tactics will get you nowhere." But she did pick one of those delicious-looking brownies. Yep, this brownie and those cupcakes she'd eaten from Jewel would surely go to her waist, but hey, she only had one life to live and she was going to live it by eating whatever she wanted during her the Christmas season. After all, that's what New Year's was made for. Resolutions. She'd get some heavy-duty skiing in for exercise come the New Year.

A momentary shiver of remembrance raced through Rachel as visions of almost being caught in an avalanche last year played havoc in her head. Jaxie had swallowed by it and had almost died. It had been a jolt to her best friend and herself. A wake-up call that you only lived once, so it was best to live out your intimate fantasies while you were alive.

"I need to know how you found out," Rachel said. The question was literally burning through her now.

"Well...we kind of sensed something when we were in the cab on the way back from the airport and we mentioned the Santa-themed ménage night," Rob said slowly.

"And then, in your new office, how you were watching that Santa keychain..." Ron continued. He gazed over at Rob, who shrugged his shoulders as if to say that was all there was to it.

Bullshit.

"Okay, spill it. There's more. I can read it in your eyes. How did you know I was coming here tonight? No one knew, unless Jewel somehow figured it out and told you?"

Both men shook their heads.

"Sophie somehow figured it out?"

They shook their heads again.

"How the hell did you know I was coming here? Ava had no clue. I told her I was under the weather and she had no problem taking over tonight. So how did you know?"

They simply stared at her, their gazes scorching her to the point she wanted to whip off the comforter. But no. Why should she give them a free show when they were holding back? She just knew they were.

Frustration burned deeper and Rachel shifted uneasily on the chaise. She wanted to stomp her feet and pout, but that would be immature, wouldn't it?

"Who told you to come to the airport to pick me up?"

They didn't answer her question.

Damn!

"You are so cute when you're upset. Isn't she, Ron?" Rob said with a teasing grin. He held out the plate again, offering her more of those irresistible goodies.

"Absolutely adorable," Ron answered with a wink.

For a moment, Rachel almost buckled into her weakness of having another one of those delicious brownies and suddenly she realized the power she had over them. They would tell her or else...

She smiled. Yeah, they would tell her.

"Uh oh." Rob suddenly tensed.

"Yeah, I will echo that, bro. She's smiling and in a way of the cat about to eat the canary," Ron said slowly.

"No one is going to eat anyone until I get answers."

They got her meaning, and they both swore beneath their breaths.

Inwardly, Rachel pumped her fist in the air in victory. She had them by the balls, so to speak. Oh, she liked this feminine power.

"We can't tell you...we promised," Rob said. He had a sudden look of desperation in his gaze.

"I'm sure she'll understand if we break the promise," Ron said. "I mean, Rach is giving us no choice. I, for one, don't want a wall up between us. I want to love her. Make love to her. Be with her."

Rachel couldn't believe what Ron was saying. It was as if she suddenly wasn't even here as they spoke to each other. Or maybe they were just open kind of guys, and truly did care for her?

They want to love me? That concept just didn't seem to sink in.

"Who is she? Who did you promise?" she prodded.

Who the hell knew about her fetish? It just was not possible. She'd guarded her secret, telling no one but...

"Oh. My. Gosh," she whispered beneath her breath.

The guys stiffened as she looked up at them.

Damn her! She'd never expected that Jaxie would look at her personal journals. But it all made sense now, why she was throwing a Santa Fetish Ménage evening. It was for her and Jaxie had even told these two.

"You won't have to betray her, because I think I suddenly figured it all out. The only one who had access to my house was Jaxie. She sent you to pick me up and she read my diaries."

Both men looked puzzled.

"You have diaries?" Ron asked.

Darn, another of her secrets was out.

"I bet they'll be interesting reading. We can find out all her deepest, darkest desires," Rob grinned.

There was a teasing glint to his gaze, but there was also a seriousness there as well. He would read them. The idea of Rob and Ron actually reading her intimate fantasies should have freaked her out. It didn't. She wanted them to. Then they could do all those wicked things to her that she'd fantasized about.

"You boys have been very naughty in playing matchmaker with Jaxie. Very naughty indeed." Rachel had wanted to keep her voice stern and inject disappointment, but her words came out husky.

Her secret was out and the sky had not fallen. It was as if a huge burden had been lifted. It was...freeing.

"Naughty boys should be punished," she stated.

Once again, her voice was too darned husky.

"Naughty boys love to punish naughty girls. Two of us against one of you, sweetheart. We win," Rob said in a strangled voice.

Arousal coursed through Rachel. The idea of them dominating her, taking her...it excited her. Just as much as Santa thrilled her. Maybe more.

Oh dear. Had she just discovered another fetish for herself? She'd loved being tied up on the bed. Loved what they'd done to her.

The room had fallen silent as the two men stared at her. Their gazes were serious. Hungry. Seriously hungry.

Ron placed the dish of goodies back upon the cart and Rob held out his hand to her.

"Leave the comforter. We just want you and only you. Always," he said.

Rachel swallowed as tingles of anticipation swept through her.

For a moment, Rachel's shyness almost won out and she hesitated on removing the protectiveness of the comforter cocooning her. But she gathered her courage and whipped it aside.

Both men inhaled.

Rob nodded to his extended hand and wiggled his fingers to her.

"Come with us," he whispered.

"Always," she whispered back. She meant it. Suddenly there were no other men for her in this lifetime. Just these two.

Rachel's fingers trembled as she placed them into Rob's palm. He pulled her from the chaise with ease and as she stood before him, he suddenly lifted her into his arms.

Ron had the shower already running. Steam wafted out of the large stall and curled around Rob and Rachel as he carried her in. Ron stood there beneath the jets of spray. His gaze was dark with desire. He was fully naked, and muscles rippled across his chest and biceps as he sheathed a condom on his huge erection. She noted a large open package of condoms and a tube of lube on the soap shelf.

"It seems we'll be in here for a while," she said softly as Rob placed her onto her feet. Shivers of anticipation rippled through her as the warm water curled around her toes. Without warning Ron grabbed her by her hands and dragged her beneath the spray with him.

The jets of water pummeled her shoulders and back. It felt good, like she was being massaged. as he faced her toward him.

"I need you," he whispered. He nodded for her to look up at the ceiling. She did and gasped.

A ball of mistletoe hung above them. But that's not what made her gasp. It was the other thing that dangled there. A chain dripped from a trolley-like contraption in the ceiling. On the other end of the chain, partially hidden behind the shower curtain, were black leather wrist restraints, similar to the ones she'd had on while in bed.

Her breath backed up as arousal flared. They were going to restrain her. In here.

"Two against one, baby," Rob said as he stepped into the shower behind her and grabbed a condom off the shelf.

"Restrain away," she said. Her breaths came faster at the flare of excitement in Ron's eyes as he reached for the cuffs. The tinkle of chains erupted above the splash of running water and before Rachel knew it, her wrists were cuffed and pulled high up over her head and then Ron was leaning closer to her.

"I've been dying to do this again, sweetness, and we'll be taking full advantage of the mistletoe," Ron murmured.

His lips parted and she closed her eyes.

Rachel moaned as Ron's mouth locked onto hers. The impact of his hard kiss twirled wicked sensations through her. His tongue boldly pushed past her teeth and mated with her own tongue, sending exquisite shockwaves right down to the tips of her toes. His lips were soft, yet firm. His tongue solid and sure as he explored her cavern, the feel of his probing had her blood pumping heat and excitement through her.

Behind her, Rob's hands swept over her waist. He held her firm and she tensed at his thick erection pressing against her sphincter. His mouth nestled near her earlobe. His five-o'-clock shadow erotically scratched her neck and his hot breath caressed her cheek.

"Just relax," he said into her ear.

Easy for him to say, he wasn't the one getting a cock sliding into his ass or his mouth fucked by a mind-wrenching kiss.

She inhaled and forced herself to calm. Okay, she could do this.

Rob's lubed shaft sunk into her. It was a thick column that stretched into her like nothing ever had. Her anal muscles protested and clenched and then gave in, allowing him to enter deeper. Pinpricks of pleasure-pain gripped along her muscles. She gasped at the intrusion. She liked it.

Oh. This is different. This is nice.

Rachel kissed Ron back and delicately pushed her hips backward to see how it felt for Rob's shaft to go deeper. The fullness had her moaning into Ron's mouth. He kissed her harder. She pulled at her restraints as her senses spun and a dark haze whispered through her making her lose any semblance of self-control.

She moaned and bucked between them.

"Easy, baby. Easy. Nice and slow," Rob growled against her ear, his hands tightened at her waist.

Rachel's mind whirled. Her body protested at the slowness.

She whimpered. It was a lost sound. A desperate noise.

Without breaking the kiss, Ron moved closer, his shaft rubbing against her clit. Spirals of pleasure wrapped around her. She pulled against her restraints again as the pleasure storm began to build.

Rob sunk into her deeper. She heard him sigh as he stayed inside her for a pulse pounding moment, then he withdrew and pushed into her again. His penis throbbed every time he entered her and in seconds he began a slow, teasing rhythm.

He withdrew and Ron broke the kiss. She whimpered her distress, but neither man said anything as they eased her backward a few steps until the warm water was splashing over her head.

A second later, Ron lifted her right leg and she cried out as his silky length came into her, hard and fast.

"You're mine," Ron growled after he broke the kiss.

"And mine," Rob agreed.

Wow, these guys were incredible. They were in love with her, and she'd had no clue. For a moment those thoughts overwhelmed Rachel, but they disintegrated as Ron withdrew and impaled her again, shocking pleasure through her.

He pulled out and Rob sunk into her.

Suddenly she became aware of every sound they made. Their erotic grunts and sensual groans. The harsh slap of their flesh as they took turns thrusting into her. And she became very aware of the loving way Rob's hands held her waist and how Ron's hands slid up and down her sides in a slow, comforting rhythm. His caresses glided over her skin like a ribbon of silk. Their scents, dark, musky and mysterious. Identical yet different.

Their cocks pistoned into her like thick jolts of lightning, pushing her closer and closer to the edge with their every deliberate thrust. Her thighs tightened. Her pussy and ass clenched around the slippery intruders.

Ron's mouth slanted over hers again.

It was exactly what she needed to slip into the killing pleasure that suddenly swallowed her whole. She arched into Ron, then bucked backward against Rob as the delicious shudders hit. She convulsed and cried out as the spasms ripped her apart.

She knew they spoke the truth.

Now she belonged to both of them. She was *theirs.*

Epilogue

TWO NIGHTS LATER, CHRISTMAS Eve

"Come on, push, Jaxie! One more time. Just one more time!" Dr. Kelsie Madison shouted.

Rachel tensed as she watched Jaxie bear down. Her face was red. Perspiration drenched her face and glistened in her tangled hair, but Rachel swore Jaxie had never looked more beautiful.

Ewan and Royce stood on each side of Jaxie, their faces alternating between concern every time Jaxie cried out and then happiness when she calmed in between the quickening contractions.

Jaxie had called her early this morning, telling her to come and be with her when she gave birth. When Rachel had been in Europe, Jaxie had insisted when the time drew near, that Rachel had to be with her. That had been another reason she'd come back.

Rachel hadn't told Jaxie about her getting together with Ron and Rob. Or that both men were moving in with her. Actually they were moving in right at this moment and the minute she was assured that Jaxie and the baby were safe and healthy, she was going to go home to her very own men. Then they would trim the Christmas tree.

Rachel smiled as Jaxie caught her gaze and bore down one more time.

"Push," Kelsie urged. And then, just like that, the doctor pulled the baby free and efficiently cut and tied the umbilical cord.

An irritated wail quickly erupted. It was followed by a flurry of awed whispers from Ewan and Royce, along with squeals of delight from Jaxie who held out her arms in angst wanting to hold her newborn.

"You have a baby boy. Congratulations," Kelsie said as she handed the baby to the nurse who quickly cleaned him and wrapped him in a snug flannel blanket.

"And he looks very healthy," the doctor said. "You can have a few minutes and then we'll check him out to make sure all is good. But I see no problems."

The nurse placed the baby on Jaxie's chest and then she and the doctor left the room.

Rachel's heart burst with love at the sight of the newborn. His chubby face was red, his eyes scrunched tight, and his plump little fingers curled into fists as he wailed. She noted right away that he had Jaxie's nose and Ewan's strong chin.

The baby quietened as soon as Jaxie held him.

"Whoa there, she's a natural mama," Royce grinned as he crouched beside the bed and looked at Jaxie and the baby. Love shone quite clearly in his eyes.

"She's the most beautiful mama in the world," Ewan whispered as he leaned over and gently rubbed his thumb beneath the baby's chin.

To everyone's surprise, the baby uncurled his right hand and swiftly grabbed Ewan's thumb.

"Wow, what a grip!" Ewan said with a chuckle. He was also gazing at Jaxie with love in his eyes.

Jaxie smiled at both of her men and then gazed back down at her baby.

"And I'm the happiest mama in the world. I've never seen such a beautiful, perfect baby."

Rachel bit her bottom lip as tears of joy bubbled for her best friend. As Ewan and Royce hovered around Jaxie, her friend gave Rachel a wink and Rachel took the opportunity to wave goodnight.

Jaxie nodded, thankfully not protesting as Rachel let herself out of the room.

This was Jaxie's family time and Rachel didn't want to intrude.

Besides, she had her own family now waiting for her at home, and suddenly she couldn't wait to get there because she had her own two perfect men waiting for her.

The cold late-December air blew against her face as she stepped outside of the hospital and walked toward the parking lot.

Rachel smiled. Santa had been really good to her this Christmas. He'd given her the two sexiest hunks in the world, and now she was going home to her two men and have them make love to her beneath the Christmas tree that they were putting up tonight in her living room.

Home sweet home never felt so good.

The End Want more Jan Springer Adult Romances?

Mini Catalog

Kidnap Fantasies Series

In the land of the rich and famous, the top-secret Kidnap Fantasies is the answer to discreet and naughty downtime.

Book One

Jade's Fantasy

When ex-downhill skier Jade's two sisters give her a Kidnap Fantasies questionnaire, Jade is aroused at the prospect of having no-strings fun in the sun with a stranger whose only job would be to fulfill her every intimate fantasy. Although she knows she's too shy to send it in, she secretly pours her deepest wishes into the questionnaire.

Soon the questionnaire mysteriously vanishes and Jade's fantasy man appears on her luxury yacht in the form of a sexy handy man who gives her an intimate toy-filled holiday she'll never forget.

Book Two
Christmas Lovers
(can also be found in the Merry Ménage Kisses Boxed Set)
Sergeant Connor Jordan, wounded overseas and sent back to the States to recuperate, just cannot stop fantasizing about the sexy nurse who cared for him. When his brothers give him a holiday gift certificate to Kidnap Fantasies, a top-secret fantasy organization, Connor knows he'll use their gift, if only to help him forget his wickedly delicious attraction to Nurse Sparks.
Nurse Tania Sparks has always been purely professional with her injured soldiers...until sinfully sexy Connor Jordan enters her hospital. He makes her body throb with an intense desire she's never known before.

The last thing she wants is to get involved with the injured warrior. So what's a woman supposed to do to relieve her naughty frustrations? Call Kidnap Fantasies and have them supply her with a look-alike man who'll help her forget her sexy soldier...

When Tania and Connor unexpectedly come together at a secluded mountain chalet, their love explodes in a ménage of passion, sensuous desires and a happily forever after.

Contains ménage scenes.

Book Three

Zero to Sexy

Because Santana hides from something bad in his past he lives only for the moment and doesn't dare dream of a future. He exists within the sensual world of Kidnap Fantasies, a top-secret escort world where he explores his sexuality and enjoys pleasure with both men and women. But it is love at first sight the instant he sees Amy at his good friend's wedding. She's got future written all over her. He knows she is a hunger he must deny, so why is he whispering "you're mine" to her at the wedding?

The instant Amy Sparks sees the handsome African American at her sister's wedding, she knows in her heart that he's everything she's ever fantasized about in a lover, but before they can connect, he mysteriously disappears. Upon discovering he works for Kidnap Fantasies, she knows how he'll make all her intimate fantasies come true...

When Santana's next Kidnap Fantasies assignment turns out to be Amy, he knows he must protect her from his past and he can be with her only this one time...

Reader Advisory: Includes a sizzling ménage scene and some male on male sensual interaction.

Boxed Sets

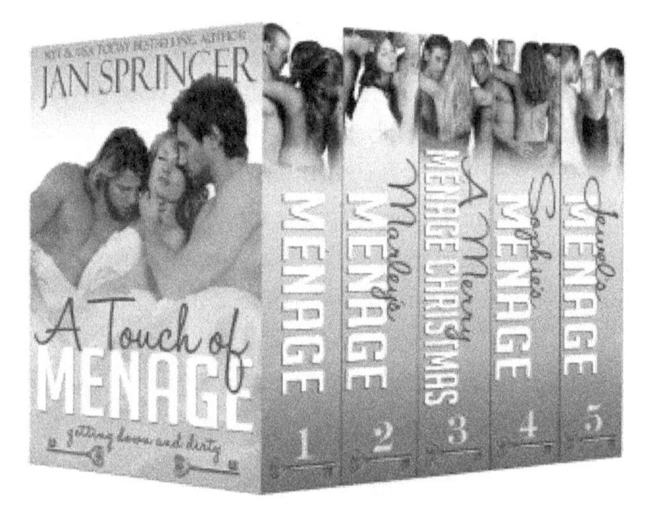

SIX Erotic Romance Ménage Stories! INCLUDES A BONUS MÉNAGE EBOOK

Step into The Key Club's Ménage Nights where naughty fantasies come true and two men are hotter than one. Includes FIVE bestselling The Key Club stories; Ménage, Marley's Ménage, A Merry Ménage Christmas, Sophie's Ménage and Jewel's Ménage.

BONUS Ménage BOOK "Cowboys for Christmas" book 1 of Jan's new Cowboys Online series. Jennifer Jane is getting THREE Cowboys for Christmas ~ What more could a girl want?

Jennifer Jane Watson has spent the past ten Christmases in a maximum-security prison. The last thing she expects is to get early parole along with a job on a secluded Canadian cattle ranch serving Christmas holiday dinners to three of the sexiest cowboys she's ever met!

Pleasure Bound Box Set

The Complete Series

Books 1 - 6

A Futuristic Adult Romance

Books 1-6

This PLEASURE BOUND BOXED SET is an EROTIC ROMANCE and includes the first SIX books in the Pleasure Bound series.

TOP-SECRET MISSION: Explore a recently discovered planet in outer space.

DISCOVERY: A sizzling trip into the realms of bondage, bdsm, pleasure-pain, betrayal and...love.

Inside this Boxed Set:

During a top-secret mission to a newly discovered planet, the six Hero siblings are thrust into a sensual world of erotic violence, unconventional romance and sizzling sex.

A HERO'S WELCOME

Pleasure Bound Book One

Jan Springer

Being shot and held captive isn't what astronaut Joe Hero had in mind when he agreed to a top-secret mission to explore a newly discovered planet for NASA.

But a man would have to be dead not to fall for the sensual female doctor in charge of his care.

One night of scorching passion in the arms of the stranger from another planet is enough to convince Dr. Annie there's more to males than she's been taught by the Educators.

Who is this sexy hunk and why does she welcome him into her bed and her heart every chance she gets?

A HERO ESCAPES

Pleasure Bound Book Two

Jan Springer

Queen Jacey has always fantasized about bedding a male.

But taking one for her enjoyment is strictly forbidden. That is, until an attractive well-hung stranger from another planet forces her to overcome her training and her beliefs.

Being held captive and forced to mate with a gorgeous Queen isn't exactly what astronaut Ben Hero expected when he agreed to explore a newly discovered planet for NASA.

Escaping should be his top priority but making sizzling love to Jacey is all he can think about.

When he discovers she's also being held captive, Ben's protective instincts kick in big time.

Suddenly they're on the run, irresistibly aroused, and wrapped in each other's arms every chance they get!

A HERO BETRAYED

Pleasure Bound Book Three

Jan Springer

Astronaut Buck Hero didn't count on being held captive or becoming infected with passion poison when he agreed to explore a newly discovered planet for NASA.

If he doesn't get the cure soon he's going to be one very dead man.

Fugitive on-the-run Virgin has just rescued an infected male and needs to administer the cure - a twenty-four-hour sex marathon. Then she'll turn him over to his enemies in order to gain her freedom.

But her well-laid plans go into orbit when she discovers she's fallen in love with the stranger from another world.

A HERO'S KISS

Pleasure Bound Book Four

Jan Springer

During a secret NASA mission to locate their brothers on the faraway planet of Paradise, the Hero sisters become separated after they crash land...and find unexpected romance with the tormented male warriors of the species.

Jarod and Piper

Being injured and infected by sensuous swamp water isn't what Piper Hero signed up for when she agreed to search for her three missing brothers. But when she's rescued by a dangerously sexy man who makes her so hot that she can't even think straight, Piper is glad that she came.

Jarod Ellis has sworn off women. But he's captivated by Piper Hero, a woman who claims to be related to the Earthmen he has vowed to protect with his life. Although he mistrusts her, she sets free a carnal inferno of needs he's never experienced during his previous life as a pleasure slave.

Despite her intimate fantasies coming true, Piper knows she needs to continue her mission of reuniting her siblings and she'll do it-with or without the help of her well-hung stud...

A HERO WANTED

Pleasure Bound Book Five

(Loosely connected with this series)

Jan Springer

Old-fashioned gal needs a man who loves to walk in the rain. Must be well-hung. A homebody, white picket fence-type of guy. Sexual requirements-gentle yet untamed lover. He must be sexually adventurous who will train me to be same. Must be romantic, enjoy toys, interested in mutual light bondage, ménages are welcome.

That's what full-figured, antiques shop owner Jenna MacLean wants when she and her best friend outline a want ad just for fun on their weekly girls' night out.

After years of being away from his pretty-plus sized ex-girlfriend, Sully's back in town. When he finds the want ad, he knows he's the only man who can make all of Jenna's sizzling-hot fantasies come true.

She's never left his heart and he needs her back in his bed-but he's not going the traditional romantic route. This time, he'll prove he loves her with help from the notorious Ménage Club, a relationship club designed specifically to get estranged couples back together with the help of a third and sometimes a fourth in the bedroom.

CAPTIVE HEROES

Pleasure Bound Book Six

Jan Springer

During a secret NASA mission to locate their brothers on the faraway planet of Paradise, the Hero sisters become separated after they crash land...and find unexpected romance with the tormented alien male warriors of the species in this ultra-long scifi book.

Taylor and Kayla

While searching for her brothers, Kayla Hero is bound and imprisoned by the Breeders— along with a male captive whose tantalizing scars pique her interest. Forced to escape with him, she's irresistibly aroused when she suddenly becomes his captive.

Wild lust flares in Kayla's eyes— a sensual side effect of the Fever Swamp water she's accidentally ingested. Taylor knows he will enjoy administering the cure — lots of sizzling hot lovemaking!

Blackie and Kinley

Injured and lost in a dense jungle, Kinley Hero is intimidated by the scarred man who hunts her, especially due to the power of erotic submission he holds over her.

Capturing his beautiful female prey, Blackie can't wait to train her as a pleasure slave for the Death Valley Boys. When her captor slips a collar around her neck, Kinley must struggle with lust as a natural submissive.

SHADES OF
MENAGE
JAN SPRINGER
JUDE OUTLAW 1
THE CLAIMING 2
PERFECT 3
IMPERFECT 4

Shades of Ménage Boxed Set: Four Book Romance Ménage Collection

A fast-acting virus has killed a majority of the world's female population. Women's rights are stripped away and The Claiming Law is created, allowing groups of men to stake a claim on a female—as their sensual property.

After five years of fighting in the Terrorist Wars, the Outlaw brothers are coming home to declare ownership on the women they love...and they'll do it any way they can in Jude Outlaw and The Claiming.

PLUS

In the future...for population control, each human is embedded with a microchip that suppresses the urge to mate.

Centuries later,...A rebel group of young doctors are secretly tampering with their microchips and experimenting with intimacy. Now they search for allies who can help them with their cause – to eventually free humanity in the Dystopian Romance Ménage stories "Perfect" & "Imperfect".

A CONTEMPORARY EROTIC ROMANCE BOXED SET

Naughty Girl Desires Boxed Set: Romance, Contemporary Romance, Romance Suspense, Box Set

(m/f only)

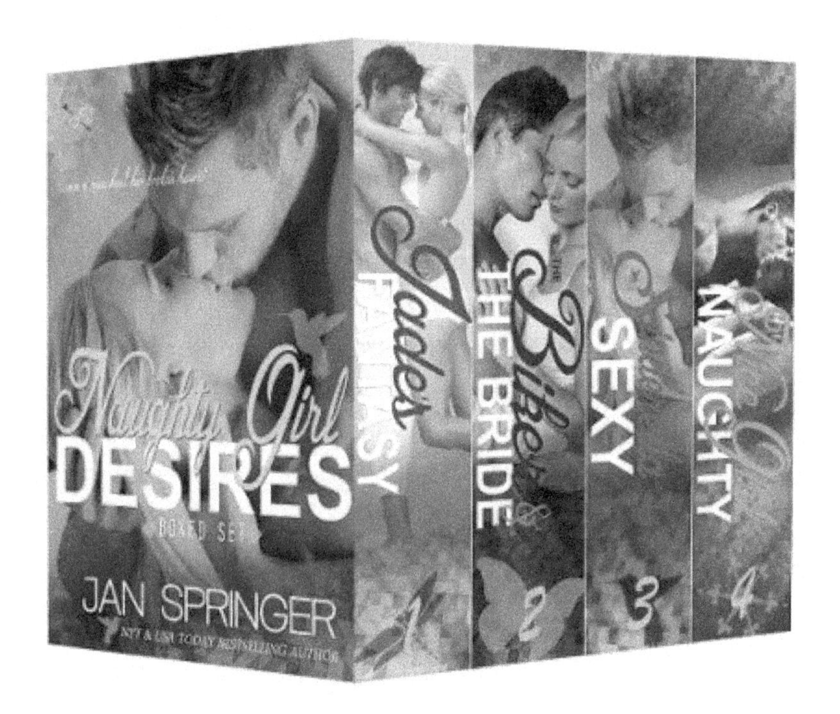

What You'll Find Inside Naughty Girl Desires

Jade's Fantasy

Kidnap Fantasies 1

Jan Springer

In the land of the rich and famous, Kidnap Fantasies is the answer to discreet naughty downtime.

When ex-downhill skier Jade Hart's two sisters give her a Kidnap Fantasies questionnaire, Jade is aroused at the prospect of having no-strings fun in the sun with a stranger whose only job would be to fulfill her every intimate fantasy. Although she knows she's too shy to send it in, she secretly pours her deepest wishes into the questionnaire.

Soon the questionnaire mysteriously vanishes and Jade's fantasy man appears on her luxury yacht in the form of a sexy handy man who gives her an intimate toy-filled Christmas holiday she'll never forget.

The Biker and The Bride
Jan Springer

Wrapped in red-hot lust for revenge, Avery plots to murder the man responsible for the death of her son. Her plans are dashed when her ex-husband crashes her wedding and whisks her away on his motorcycle to the rustic Canadian wilderness cabin they'd once honeymooned. Police detective, Mason is fighting for Avery's love with everything he has.

Armed with whipped cream, handcuffs and his undying devotion, Mason vows he will make Avery love again. But it's only a matter of time before the man she'd planned to kill hunts them down...

Sinderella Sexy
Jan Springer

By day, she's a dedicated gynecologist.

By night, Dr. Ella Cinder, escapes reality by secretly performing in her own erotic, adult version of Cinderella, aptly re-titled Sinderella. When sexy colleague Dr. Roarke Stephenson shows up in the Sinderella audience on the same night her Prince Charming stands her up, Ella seizes the opportunity to make Roarke into her Prince Charming for one carnal night of extremely naughty fun in front of an audience. But at the strike of midnight, Ella knows she must face the harsh reality that Roarke must never learn her secret life and they can never be together again. Until then, she'll make sure he'll never forget their night of sensual play.

Dr. Roarke Stephenson is immediately captured by the lusciously curvy actress who hides behind a mask and is known only as Sinderella. For some insane reason she reminds him of his klutzy co-worker, Ella. But that's not possible. Ella would never have the nerve to do the wickedly delicious things Sinderella does to him, or would she?

Nice Girl Naughty

Jan Springer

Blind since nineteen, Summer has blossomed into a famous wood carver. When she's almost killed by a serial killer, she's whisked away to a secluded wilderness cabin by the man she once secretly loved.

Summer can't get enough of touching professional bodyguard Nick Cassidy's thick, powerful muscles and all those other hard, yummy male body parts that she has always longed to explore.

For years Nick has stayed away from his best friend's kid sister, nice girl Summer. Now he's back, and sweeping his gorgeous redhead into the naughty cravings he's always had for her. With passion blinding him, Nick doesn't realize their hideout isn't safe—until it's too late.

Please note: The titles in Naughty Girl Desires have been previously published.

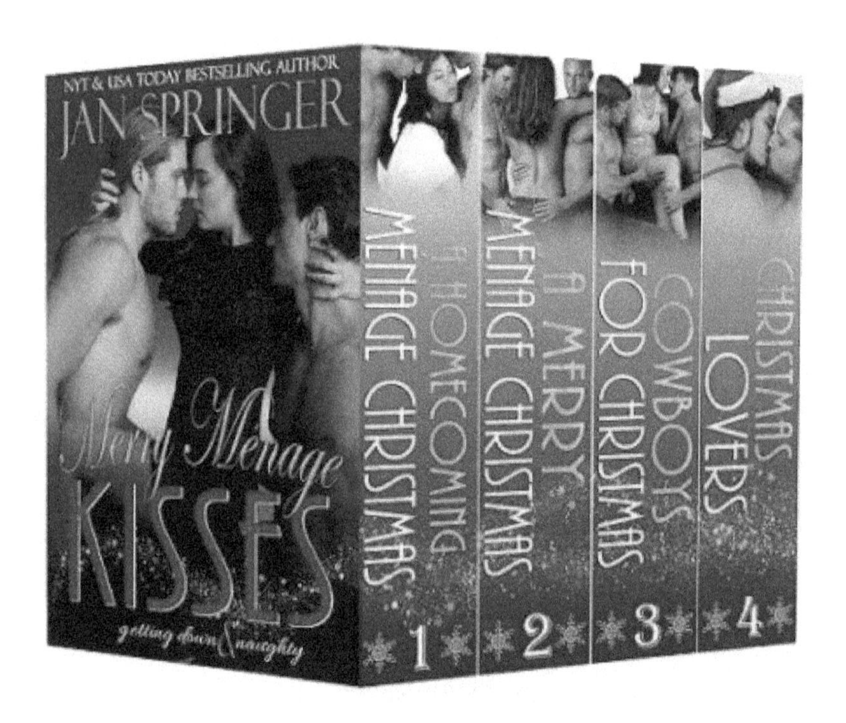

What You'll Find In The

Merry Ménage Kisses Boxed Set

Wrap yourself in four sexy holiday themed adult romance ménages.

A Homecoming Ménage Christmas

Jan Springer

Rachel has a very naughty secret and she's way too embarrassed to let anyone know about it. When The Key Club throws a Santa Fetish Ménage Night it's almost too good to be true. She has to figure out how to participate without anyone finding out!

Key Club bartenders Rob and Ron Simpson have fallen head over Santa hats for quiet, nice girl Rachel. But she has no clue how they feel about her. But she will know, because Rachel is coming home from a trip to Europe and the twin brothers are going to give her the best Homecoming Ménage Christmas ever. They'll do it with the help of some naughty toys, the Red Room, a safe word and...Santa Claus.

A Merry Ménage Christmas

Jan Springer

Dr. Kelsie Madison can't remember the last time she's had no-strings sex and that's her clue she's been working way too hard. It's time to unwind at the Key Club by indulging in a yummy Christmas present for herself. Something she's never experienced before - a red-hot ménage.

ER Dr. Ryder Greene and his roommate, physiotherapist, Dixon Flynn love sharing their women. They've had their eye on cute Dr. Kelsie Madison for quite some time, but she's a workaholic and she never has time to play.

When they learn she'll be at the Santa Claus Ménage Night festivities, they'll make sure they're the ones kissing Kelsie under the mistletoe. And if they get their wish, Kelsie will be taking them home for Christmas.

Cowboys for Christmas

Jan Springer

Jennifer Jane (JJ) Watson has spent the past ten Christmases in a maximum-security prison.

The last thing she expects is to get early parole, along with a job on a remote Canadian cattle ranch serving Christmas holiday dinners to three of the sexiest cowboys she's ever met!

Rafe, Brady and Dan thought they were getting a couple of male ex-cons to help out around their secluded ranch, but instead they get an attractive and very appealing female.

In the snowbound wilds of Northern Ontario, female companionship is rare.

It's a good thing the three men like to share...

They're dominating, sexy-as-sin and they fill JJ with the hottest ménage fantasies she's ever had. Suddenly she's craving cowboys for Christmas and wishing for something she knows she can never have...a happily ever after.

Christmas Lovers

Jan Springer

Sergeant Connor Jordan, wounded overseas and sent back to the States to recuperate, just cannot stop fantasizing about the sexy nurse who cared for him. When his brothers give him a holiday gift certificate to Kidnap Fantasies, a top-secret fantasy organization, Connor knows he'll use their gift, if only to help him forget his wickedly delicious attraction to Nurse Sparks.

Nurse Tania Sparks has always been purely professional with her injured soldiers...until sinfully sexy Connor Jordan enters her hospital. He makes her body throb with an intense desire she's never known before. The last thing she wants is to get involved with the injured warrior. So what's a woman supposed to do to relieve her naughty frustrations? Call Kidnap Fantasies and have them supply her with a look-alike man who'll help her forget her sexy soldier...

When Tania and Connor unexpectedly come together at a secluded mountain chalet, their love explodes in a ménage of passion, sensuous desires and a happily forever after.

Contains ménage scenes.

For more Jan Springer stories, please visit http://www.janspringer.com

---

Jan's Newsletter

Hi! If you would like to get an email when my books are released, you can sign up here:

Newsletter: http://ymlp.com/xguembmugmgb

Your emails will never be shared and you can unsubscribe whenever you like.

About the Author

Jan Springer writes full-time at her home nestled in cottage country, Ontario, Canada. She enjoys hiking, kayaking, gardening, reading and writing. She is a member of the Writers Union of Canada, Romance Writers of America. She loves hearing from her readers.

A Word From The Author

Hi! Thank you for purchasing this book. Word of mouth is important for any author to succeed. If you enjoyed this story feel free to leave a short review at the place where you bought it. I would really appreciate it. I look forward to bringing you more stories in the near future. Thanks!

If you would like to contact me or personally send me feedback, you can reach me by using my contact page at: http://janspringerauthor.wordpress.com/

contact/

Here are other ways we can connect:

Jan Springer Website at http://www.janspringer.com
Facebook - https://www.facebook.com/janspringereroticromance
Twitter - https://twitter.com/janspringer @janspringer
Pinterest - http://www.pinterest.com/janspringer1/
Jan's Blog - http://janspringerauthor.wordpress.com/blog-2/
LinkedIn - http://ca.linkedin.com/in/janspringerauthor/
Google Plus - https://plus.google.com/u/0/101527334949931513035/posts
Jan's Newsletter - http://ymlp.com/xguembmugmgb
Goodreads - https://www.goodreads.com/author/show/260628.Jan_Springer

Happy Reading,
jan springer